Welcome to the world of
St Piran's Hospital—

Next to the rugged shores of Penhally Bay
lies the picturesque Cornish town of St Piran,
where you'll find a bustling hospital famed
for the dedication, talent and passion
of its staff—on and off the wards!

Under the warmth of the Cornish sun,
Italian doctors, heart surgeons and
playboy princes discover that romance blossoms
in the most unlikely of places…

You'll also meet the devilishly handsome
Dr Josh O'Hara and the beautiful,
fragile Megan Phillips…and discover the secret
that tore these star-crossed lovers apart.

Turn the page to step into St Piran's—
where every drama has a dreamy doctor…
and a happy ending.

Dear Reader

Having written SPANISH DOCTOR, PREGNANT MIDWIFE, based in Penhally Bay, I was delighted to be asked to contribute to the new series set in and around St Piran's Hospital.

I was especially pleased to spend some time with the characters on the rugged coast of Cornwall, a part of the world I love, and which is very similar to the West Coast of Scotland where I live now.

This is the story of extreme sport fanatic Mac, who is a doctor with the Royal Cornwall Air Ambulance Service, and Abby, single mum and air ambulance paramedic.

When committed bachelor Mac meets Abby he is immediately attracted to her. Soon after he finds out that Abby has a secret that is about to turn his life upside down, and he learns that loving involves taking risks too.

I hope you enjoy reading Mac and Abby's story, and would love to hear from you—my blog is on the eHarlequin website: www.eharlequin.com

Anne Fraser

ST PIRAN'S: DAREDEVIL, DOCTOR...DAD!

BY
ANNE FRASER

First published in Great Britain 2011
Harlequin Mills & Boon Limited,
Eton House, 18-24 Paradise Road, Richmond, Surrey TW9 1SR

© Harlequin Books S.A. 2011

ISBN: 978 0 263 88578 1

Special thanks and acknowledgement are given to Anne Fraser
for her contribution to the *St Piran's Hospital* series

Harlequin Mills & Boon policy is to use papers that are natural,
renewable and recyclable products and made from wood grown in
sustainable forests. The logging and manufacturing process conform
to the legal environmental regulations of the country of origin.

Printed and bound in Spain
by Litografia Rosés, S.A., Barcelona

Anne Fraser was born in Scotland, but brought up in South Africa. After she left school she returned to the birthplace of her parents, the remote Western Islands of Scotland. She left there to train as a nurse, before going on to university to study English Literature. After the birth of her first child she and her doctor husband travelled the world, working in rural Africa, Australia and Northern Canada. Anne still works in the health sector. To relax, she enjoys spending time with her family, reading, walking and travelling.

Recent titles by the same author:

PRINCE CHARMING OF HARLEY STREET
RESCUED: MOTHER AND BABY
MIRACLE: MARRIAGE REUNITED
SPANISH DOCTOR, PREGNANT MIDWIFE*

*The Brides of Penhally Bay

ST PIRAN'S HOSPITAL
*Where every drama has a dreamy doctor…
and a happy ending.*

*In December we gave you the first two St Piran's stories
in one month!*

**Nick Tremayne and Kate Althorp
finally got their happy-ever-after in:**
ST PIRAN'S: THE WEDDING OF THE YEAR
by Caroline Anderson

**Dr Izzy Bailey was swept off her feet
by sexy Spaniard Diego Ramirez:**
ST PIRAN'S: RESCUING PREGNANT CINDERELLA
by Carol Marinelli

**In January the arrival of sizzlingly hot
Italian neurosurgeon Giovanni Corezzi
was enough to make any woman forget the cold!**
ST PIRAN'S: ITALIAN SURGEON, FORBIDDEN BRIDE
by Margaret McDonagh

**This month daredevil doc William MacNeil
unexpectedly discovers that he's a father in:**
ST PIRAN'S: DAREDEVIL, DOCTOR…DAD!
by Anne Fraser

**The new heart surgeon has everyone's pulses racing
in March**
ST PIRAN'S: THE BROODING HEART SURGEON
by Alison Roberts

Fireman Tom Nicholson steals Flora Loveday's heart in April
ST PIRAN'S: THE FIREMAN AND NURSE LOVEDAY
by Kate Hardy

**Newborn twins could just bring a May marriage miracle
for Brianna and Connor Taylor**
ST PIRAN'S: TINY MIRACLE TWINS
by Maggie Kingsley

**And playboy Prince Alessandro Cavalieri
honours St Piran's with a visit in June**
ST PIRAN'S: PRINCE ON THE CHILDREN'S WARD
by Sarah Morgan

CHAPTER ONE

ABBY sank onto the sofa transfixed by what was happening on the TV screen. At the end of a rope, a man was being lowered out of a Royal Navy helicopter. Abby held her breath as the figure swirled precariously in the buffeting wind. She had put on the TV to catch the weather report but now she couldn't tear her eyes away from the drama unfolding in front of her.

Beneath the helicopter a boat was listing dangerously to one side, obviously in serious trouble. The reporter covering the story was telling the viewers that the Royal Navy rescue service had been called out to the stricken vessel. 'The family of four were on a sailing trip when they got into trouble off the Cornish coast. Heavy seas pushed their boat onto rocks and it is now taking on water rapidly. We have heard that the helmsman took a heavy blow to his head and is unconscious. His wife, who radioed for help, and their two young children, are still on board.'

Although the newscaster's expression was calm, Abby could detect suppressed tension in her voice. 'The helicopter crew has only a short time to get everyone off before the boat sinks. We understand that there is a doctor helping from the Royal Cornwall Air Ambulance Service.'

The man at the end of the winch dropped onto the listing boat, unhooked himself from the line and slithered his way across the deck. Within minutes he was being lifted back on board the helicopter, with two small figures attached to him like clams.

He swiftly dropped down to the boat again, retrieving another person from the stricken yacht. Heart in her mouth, Abby leaned forward. The injured skipper was still on the boat! Could he be rescued before the yacht sank, taking him and his rescuer along with it? If he had a head injury, as the newscaster was suggesting, then it would be dangerous to move him. But what other option was there? To leave him would be unthinkable.

The downdraught from the helicopter whipped the sea into a frenzy. Nearby, a coastguard rescue boat was making valiant attempts to approach the yacht but the heavy waves were preventing it from getting anywhere close. Abby squeezed her eyes closed. She could hardly bear to watch.

'A second man is being lowered onto the boat.' The newscaster's voice dropped to a whisper. 'We understand he's a doctor.'

Abby opened her eyes. Sure enough, she could just make out the letters on the fluorescent jacket of the second man.

The line attached to the helicopter was swinging wildly as the pilot struggled to keep the aircraft level. The small boat rose up to meet the man on the end of the winch then dropped away again. The figure swung first to the right then to the left as the deck kept veering away. Abby knew there was a real possibility that the rescuers might lose their own lives in the attempt to reach the injured skipper.

Suddenly the doctor was on the deck. Quickly he

released himself from the harness and the line was reeled back into the helicopter.

Almost unable to breathe, Abby watched him pick his way across the slippery deck, almost losing his balance as the boat shifted wildly in the heavy seas. Moments later another man dropped down from the helicopter, this one with a stretcher. Abby lost sight of the first man as he disappeared from view. Had he slipped overboard?

While she'd been watching, Emma had come into the room. Seeing Abby staring at the screen, she unplugged herself from her MP3 player and sat down next to her.

'Is that what you're going to be doing?' Emma asked. 'In your new job?'

'Sometimes,' Abby admitted. Although she hoped to hell she wouldn't be involved in anything quite as dangerous as what was going on in front of her. It was one thing being trained to be winched up and down from a helicopter in calm conditions—this was something altogether different.

Emma looked at her wide-eyed. 'Cool,' she said.

Thankfully her daughter didn't seem to appreciate the danger the men were in. That was good: Abby didn't want Emma worrying about her.

It seemed like hours but it could only have been a few minutes before the stretcher, now loaded with the injured skipper, was being attached to the winch. Abby knew the danger was far from over. The yacht was sinking rapidly. She was amazed that it had managed to stay afloat as long as it had.

Then the men with the stretcher were being lifted back onto the helicopter. As soon as they were on board the aircraft swung away. Seconds later the boat tipped up and with a final surge was engulfed by the waves. Any sooner and it would have taken the three men with it.

'I understand the mother and two children have been taken to hospital where they are being treated for hypothermia and shock,' the reporter continued. 'At this time we have no details about the condition of the skipper except that he is stable. But right now we can give you a live interview with some of the men involved in the daring rescue.'

The drama over, Emma went back to her music and left the room. Before Abby could switch the television off, the camera panned out slightly, revealing two men. One, a man in his fifties, was wearing the jumpsuit of the Royal Navy, the other the fluorescent jacket of a rescue doctor. Both men were smiling broadly, as if what they had just done had been exhilarating—and no more dangerous than a routine training exercise.

But as the camera zoomed closer, it was the younger man, the doctor, that made Abby's heart leap in her chest. Underneath his five-o'clock shadow there was something disturbingly familiar about his hooked nose and wide grin. But before Abby could get a better look at him the camera, frustratingly, focussed solely on his colleague.

'I have Sergeant Lightbody with me, who was the winchman involved in the rescue,' the reporter said.

The older man shifted slightly, looking uncomfortable to find himself on TV.

'Sergeant Lightbody,' the newscaster continued, 'can you tell the viewers at home what it was like out there today? From what I could see, it seemed that you just managed to get the victims off the boat in the nick of time.'

Sergeant Lightbody looked even more ill at ease. 'It was certainly a little breezy out there. I guess it was one of the more difficult situations we've been involved in for a while.'

'A little breezy? A bit of an understatement, surely? If you and your men hadn't been able to get these people off, it could've ended in tragedy. That all the family members survived is testament to the skill and courage of your team.'

'It's what we do.' Sergeant Lightbody shrugged. 'Anyway, if it hadn't been for Dr MacNeil here, we might not have got the skipper off without further injury—if at all.'

The camera shifted to the younger man. He was shaking his head. Despite the hat pulled low on his brow, shadowing his eyes, Abby realised with a jolt that she did recognise him. She didn't need to check the photograph she had kept for all these years to know that Dr MacNeil was Mac—her dead sister's lover and Emma's father!

Her legs shaking, Abby got up and retrieved the remote then froze the screen. She was breathing rapidly as she studied the fuzzy picture. It was him! He was older, yes; there were faint smile lines on either side of his mouth and radiating from the corners of his ice-blue eyes. He had filled out a little, and his hair was shorter, although still sun-bleached at the tips. Still, she would know that wide smile and glinting, expressive gaze anywhere.

She pressed the remote and the picture moved again.

'Dr MacNeil, could you tell us what happened back there? I understand you work with the Royal Cornwall Air Ambulance team. Is this just another typical day for you?'

Abby's heart was pounding so hard she could almost

hear it. She had found Mac! And not just found him, she was actually going to be working with him. She sank back down on the sofa as her legs threatened to give way beneath her. Thank God Emma had left the room. She would have known immediately that something was wrong, and right now Abby needed to make sense of what she was seeing.

Mac grinned into the camera. Unlike Sergeant Lightbody, he seemed completely at ease. 'Not exactly a typical day but, yes, the Royal Cornwall Air Ambulance teams up with other rescue services when required. We believe that having immediate medical attention on the scene can often make the difference between life and death.'

'Even if it means putting your own life at risk?' The stunning blonde reporter was almost whimpering with admiration.

'I'm pretty certain the Royal Navy wouldn't let anything happen to me,' Mac replied lightly. 'Besides, they are the real heroes. They do this sort of thing day after day. If it wasn't for the pilot of the helicopter and his team, we would have never been able to get to the casualties.'

Abby still couldn't believe what she was seeing. It was ironic, really. Abby had tried desperately to find this man years before without any success, and now he was here, in Penhally, and she'd be working with him!

Incredible to think that the reason they were here in the first place was because Emma didn't have a father.

A few months ago, just before Emma's eleventh birthday, Abby had asked her whether she wanted to invite her schoolfriends over for a party. To Abby's horror, Emma had burst into tears. When she'd eventually managed to calm her down, Emma had admitted that the children at the school had been ostracising her for the last couple of weeks. Only her best friend had still talked to her.

'But why, darling? Has something happened? You used to have loads of friends.'

Between tears and sobs of anguish Emma had explained that one of the girls had started taunting her about not having a dad.

'I told them that of course I had a dad,' Emma had said, indignant. 'So they asked where he was. When I told them I didn't know, they made fun of me. They said that I was lying or else I must be a rubbish daughter that my dad didn't want to know me. I tried to ignore them but they kept coming after me, saying these horrible things.' She'd looked up at Abby, her blue eyes swimming with tears. 'I know you're not my real mum, Mum.' She'd smiled, realising what she'd said. 'I mean, you're my real mum, but not my birth mum. But you've never told me who my father is. Why doesn't he care about me? Why *hasn't* he ever come to see me?'

Abby's heart had ached for her child. Although, as Emma had put it, *she* wasn't her biological mother, Emma was hers in every way that counted. She couldn't love her more had she given birth to her, and Emma being her twin sister Sara's child simply made the bond closer.

'I want to know who my dad is,' Emma had continued quietly. 'All the other girls at school know who their dad is, so why can't I?'

Abby had looked into the stormy blue eyes that were so like Sara's and a lump had formed in her throat. She'd known only too well how Emma had felt.

'My darling, he probably doesn't even know you exist.'

'How can he not know? How could my real mum not have told him?'

Abby winced before she'd begun speaking. 'Sara was very happy you were going to be born. I guess she didn't want to share you.'

The truth was that Sara hadn't wanted Emma's father to know about the pregnancy. At least not until she discovered that she was going to die. It was only then that she told Abby that Emma's father was Mac, the windsurfing instructor they had met while on holiday in Mykonos. When Emma was just three months old Abby went back to the Greek island to try to track him down, but it was hopeless. The summer season was over, and the visitors as well as the instructors had long since packed up and left. No one could tell her anything about Mac. Who he was or where he'd gone.

Before Sara died, Abby promised she would raise her daughter as her own. She had kept that promise and even though it hadn't always been easy, Abby had no regrets. Emma brought such joy to her life.

'I don't want to stay at that school, Mum. Please. Can't I go to a different school when I go to secondary?'

'It's not that easy, sweetie. Here in London it's difficult to find a good school within walking distance. Let me try and sort things out with the school first.'

But despite several visits to the school, the bullying continued. It both angered and saddened Abby to see Emma withdraw more and more into herself, so when Abby saw an ad for an experienced paramedic for the Royal Cornwall Air Ambulance Service, after talking it over with Emma, she decided to apply. Cornwall would be perfect for them. It was near the sea and would suit Emma's love of the outdoors much better. They were both thrilled to leave London and its sad memories behind. Abby had promised Emma that as soon as they were settled in their new home and she in her job she would continue the search for her father. Little did Abby know then that fate was going to throw them directly in his path, sooner than either of them could possibly have imagined.

Abby retrieved the tattered holiday snap from the sideboard drawer. It had been taken on the last night of her and Sara's holiday on Mykonos and Abby studied it for what must have been the hundredth time. It was a group photograph, taken on the beach. Mac had his arm draped around Sara, who was laughing up at him. She herself was at the end, a solemn figure with mid-length hair, her eyes hidden behind sunglasses. She doubted if Mac had even been aware that she was there. They had been introduced, of course, but his glance had slid almost immediately straight past Abby to her much more glamorous and fun-loving sister.

She turned to stare at the TV again, almost expecting him to reappear. She still had a week of training to complete before she started her job, so she had some time to think before she came face to face with Dr William MacNeil.

What was she going to tell Emma?

What was she going to say to Mac when they met?

What the hell was she going to do?

CHAPTER TWO

ABBY'S stomach fluttered nervously as she stepped into the base of the Royal Cornwall Air Ambulance Service. Although she had been a trained paramedic for almost twelve years, this would be an altogether different experience. She would be *flying* to rescues and despite the intensive training she had just undergone, she worried how she would cope with being lowered from a helicopter, particularly in gusty weather. But she was here now and those concerns paled into insignificance in comparison to her anxiety about meeting Mac again.

Ever since she'd seen him on television she'd been agonising over what to do. What if he was married and had a family of his own? What if Mac didn't want to know about his daughter? That hurt would be too great for the little girl. In which case should she even tell Emma that Mac was here? Did she have the right to keep the truth from Emma?

In the end she decided she wouldn't say anything to Emma until she'd had a chance to suss Mac out for herself. After all, a bad father was worse than no father at all.

The air ambulance leader, who had interviewed Abby when she'd applied for the job, met her at the door. Paul was in his early fifties with an easy smile and a relaxed and welcoming manner.

'Abby, we've been looking forward to you joining us,' he said. 'Did you enjoy your training? The course leader spoke highly of you.'

The course leader might have spoken highly of her, but that meant zilch. How she would cope in a real-life rescue would be what counted.

'What do think of Penhally Bay?' Paul continued.

'It's lovely. I haven't had too much time to explore yet—what with the course, getting my daughter settled into school and all the unpacking. But I promised Emma that on my first day off we'll have a proper look around.'

'It's a great place for a child to grow up,' Paul said. 'My kids have long since flown the coop, but they come back whenever they can. Is Emma liking Penhally High? Mine went there and they loved it. I can't imagine it's changed too much.'

Abby nodded, managing a small smile. If nothing else, their move here had been the right thing for Emma, at least as far as her new school went. Although her daughter had only been at Penhally High for a short while, she had quickly made new friends and already seemed much happier and settled.

So she was here to stay, and if life had thrown her a curve ball by flinging her directly in Mac's path, so be it. There was no going back. But until she decided what, if anything, to tell him, she would play her cards close to her chest.

Nevertheless her heart was pounding uncomfortably at the thought of meeting him again. Would he recognise her after all these years? It was unlikely. Her appearance had changed quite a bit and he hadn't paid her much attention twelve years ago. He had been far too caught up in her twin sister, the glamorous, effervescent Sara.

'Come up to the office and meet everyone,' Paul interrupted her thoughts. 'They're looking forward to meeting you.'

Her legs like jelly, Abby followed him up a steep flight of steps and into a large room where a number of people were chatting and drinking coffee.

Immediately her eyes were drawn to Mac. He was sitting, his long legs stretched out in front of him, his arms cradling the back of his head as he chatted to a colleague. Like most of the others in the room, he was dressed in an orange jumpsuit, but his was unzipped almost to the waist, revealing a dazzling white T-shirt underneath. There was no disguising his powerful build and Abby felt as if a bird were trapped in her chest.

'Everyone, I'd like you to meet our latest recruit, Abby Stevens,' Paul introduced her.

This was the moment she had been dreading. Would Mac remember her? Would he recall Sara's last name? Had he even known what it was? Although everyone turned to look at her, Abby was unable to stop herself from watching Mac's reaction. Blue eyes narrowed for a moment as if she had triggered a memory, but then he grinned and jumped to his feet. His eyes swept over her body.

'I'm Dr William MacNeil. But everyone calls me Mac.' His grip was firm and to her dismay it felt as if she had touched a live wire. Abby withdrew her hand quickly and turned to greet the other members of the team but not before she'd seen Mac's puzzled frown.

Abby forced herself to concentrate as she was

introduced to the others in the room. Apart from Paul, there were two paramedics, Mike and Jim, a pilot—an older man called Greg—as well as Lucy, another doctor, and Kirsten, whose job it was to take the calls and keep in touch with the ambulance throughout the rescue. They all smiled welcomingly.

Instinctively Abby knew she would enjoy working with this group of people—with one possible exception.

'Would you mind showing Abby around, Mac?' Paul asked. 'I have some paperwork to attend to and Lucy and Mike have just popped in to give us a report on yesterday's callout.' Paul turned to Abby. 'I'll see you all later.'

'A car accident on the coastal road,' Lucy explained as Paul left the room. She was small and plump with bright, intelligent eyes. 'The driver was going too fast for these roads and hit another car head on.'

'Any fatalities?' Abby asked.

'Surprisingly not. Luckily the oncoming car managed to swerve in time. The fire brigade had to use the jaws of life to get the driver out. It took hours and we had to keep him ventilated by hand. He's still on the critical list, but he's damned lucky to be alive.' Lucy glanced at her watch. 'Time for me to go!' She held out her hand again. 'It's good to have another woman on board, Abby. Kirsten and I get a little overwhelmed by all the testosterone around here, don't we, Kirsten?'

Kirsten grinned back. 'Don't let Lucy kid you—she's a match for the guys any time.'

Abby glanced across at Mac, who had remained silent throughout the exchange. He was studying Abby as if she puzzled him.

'Hey, have we met before?' he asked.

Abby's pulse beat even faster. Although she and Sara hadn't been identical twins there had been similarities between them—hazel eyes, straight noses and curvy mouths. But Sara had cropped her hair short and bleached it platinum blonde for their Greek holiday. In contrast, Abby had kept her shoulder length caramel hair tied back in a ponytail and at that time had worn glasses. The two sisters could hardly have looked more different and unsurprisingly Mac had barely glanced at Abby back then. Even if he did recognise her, this was hardly the time or place to tell him about Sara and Emma. Not that she had decided *what* to tell him.

She forced a smile. 'I don't think so.'

He lost the frown and grinned at her. 'You're right,' he said, lowering his voice. 'I would have remembered you. I don't tend to forget beautiful women.' He winked at her.

'And unless you're losing it, they don't tend to forget you either. That's what you mean,' chipped in Lucy. She turned to Abby, her eyes twinkling. 'Watch out for our Mac here. We love him to bits, but he's a heart-breaker. Luckily I'm too old for him and Kirsten's already taken.'

'You know I'd take you to dinner any day of the week, Lucy. Just say the word.' Mac grinned back.

'Ah, if only,' Lucy sighed theatrically. She picked up her handbag. 'I'm out of here.'

'Me too,' Kirsten said. 'I've got work to do around here!'

Left alone with Mac, Abby felt as if she had a coiled spring somewhere in her chest. He was still looking at her through half-closed eyes as if she puzzled him. 'Dr

MacNeil,' she said stiffly. 'I think we should get on with that tour, don't you?'

Again there was that heart-stopping grin. 'Call me Mac. Everyone else does.'

Mac stood back to let Abby go in front of him. He whistled under his breath as he watched the way her bottom swayed as she walked. On anyone else the orange uniform tunic top and matching trousers would have been unflattering, but it could have been tailor made for Abby. And, even apart from her figure which looked as if it had been designed with him in mind, she was a stunner. A man could drown in those eyes and as for the high cheekbones, emphasised by the hint of colour his remarks had brought to her cheeks, he had dated models who would scratch their eyes out for bone structure like that. Even the spattering of freckles over her nose didn't detract from her beauty—if anything, it made her cuter. He had already checked the third finger of her left hand. No wedding ring. Good. This was going to be interesting.

Mac had only just started showing Abby the little office where Kirsten and her small team fielded the calls when the telephone rang.

Kirsten held up a finger, asking for silence. They listened as she entered a few details into the computer.

'Try not to worry, love. We'll have someone there as soon as possible. Stay on the phone while I talk to the doctor.'

She swivelled around in her chair until she was facing Abby and Mac.

'I have a lady on the line. She's thirty-four weeks pregnant but thinks she's gone into early labour. She can't get herself to the hospital because she's on a farm and her husband is away with the car.' Kirsten covered the mouthpiece with her hand. 'She also tells me she has placenta praevia and was due to be admitted for a Caesarean section in a couple of weeks.'

'Where is the farm?' Mac asked. Gone was the laconic man of earlier. In his place was someone who was entirely focussed.

Kirsten pointed to a map. 'Over here.'

'What about the local road ambulance?' Abby asked.

Kirsten shook her head. 'It's at least an hour away on these roads and, besides, the woman—she's called Jenny Hargreaves—says the track to the farm is pretty impassable for anything except a four-by-four. We've had some heavy rain over the last fortnight.'

'We need to get her to the maternity unit as fast as possible,' Mac said. 'Okay, Kirsten, get Greg to fire the 'copter up and tell Jenny we're on our way. Is there anyone with her who can help? A friend? A neighbour?'

Kirsten shook her head. 'She's on her own, apart from her nine-year-old son.'

'Get him on the line and keep him there. Then phone St Piran's and bring them up to speed. Could you make sure we have an incubator for the baby on board, too? C'mon, Abby. I guess you're on. Let's go and get kitted up.'

As Abby raced after him down the steps and into the cloakroom where their gear was kept, she ran through what she knew about placenta praevia. And what she did know didn't make her feel any better.

'Not good news, is it?' she said as Mac passed her a jacket.

'Tell me what you know about the condition.'

'Placenta praevia is where the placenta is lying in front of the baby, blocking the birth canal. I know it can cause massive, even fatal bleeding if left untreated. If she's already in labour, we don't have much time.' Although they had covered complications of childbirth in their training, until Sara it hadn't crossed Abby's mind that it could really happen. Now she knew better. Please, God, don't let this first call end in disaster.

'Do we have an obstetrician on call?' she asked.

'At St Piran's. Kirsten will patch us through as soon as we're airborne. There's no time to wait, though.' Mac stopped for a moment and rested his hands on her shoulders. He looked directly into her eyes. 'Are you going to be okay?' His look was calm, reassuring. Everything about him radiated confidence and Abby relaxed a little.

'Sure.' She kept her voice light. 'All in a day's work.'

They piled into the helicopter and lifted off, heading towards the coast.

'ETA twenty minutes,' Greg's voice came over the radio. 'It's a bit breezy where we're heading so it might get a little bumpy.'

'Do you think we'll be able to put down?' Mac asked.

'There's a good-sized field behind the farmhouse, but I guess it depends on how soggy the ground is. We won't know until we get there.'

Abby and Mac shared a look.

'Have you ever done an emergency section before?' Abby asked. If they couldn't get mother and baby to hospital, it would be their only chance. But such a procedure would be tricky even for a qualified obstetrician in a fully equipped theatre. Her heart started pounding again. Confidence was one thing, but did Mac have the skill needed to back it up?

'I have.' He leaned across and flashed Abby another wicked grin. 'But don't worry, I have every intention of letting the obstetricians do it.' He held up a finger and listened intently.

A quiet voice came over the radio. 'Hello, Mac. Dr Gibson here. What do we have?'

'A thirty-four-weeker with placenta praevia who has gone into early labour. Control has her son on the phone. Mum tells him she thinks her contractions are coming about five minutes apart. The mother's name is Jenny Hargreaves. She tells us she was due to be delivered by section at St Piran's so you should have her case notes there.'

There was a short silence. Abby guessed Dr Gibson was bringing up Jenny's record on her computer screen.

'I'll make sure neonatal intensive care is standing by and that we have a theatre ready. How long d'you think before you'll have her here for us?'

'Another ten minutes until we land. If we can. Say another ten to examine our lady and get her loaded and twenty back. Do you think we'll make it?' Again there was that easy smile as if this was just another everyday callout.

'If anyone can, you can,' came back the reply. 'But if she's gone into active labour she could be bleeding massively and you may have to section her there and then. It won't be easy.'

'Hell, whoever said anything is easy in this job? But trust me.' He turned and winked at Abby. 'If I can get her to you without having to section her, I will.' He flexed long fingers. 'Been a long time since I did one of those.'

'Good luck,' Dr Gibson said calmly.

A short while later they reached the farm. To Abby's relief the pilot had been able to find a spot to land. The helicopter rotors had barely slowed when Mac hefted the large medical bag over his shoulder.

'Okay, we're on. Remember to keep your head down.' Abby took a deep breath, sent a silent prayer towards heaven, and followed him out of the helicopter.

Mac sprinted towards the farmhouse, carrying the medical case that weighed at least ten kilos as if it were nothing. Abby ran after him, doing her best to keep up.

A child with wide, frightened eyes was waiting for them by the doorway.

'Please hurry, my mum is bleeding,' the boy said.

This was the worst possible news. Jenny being in labour was one thing, but they had banked on having enough time to get her to hospital. If she had started bleeding it meant that the placenta was beginning to detach. As it did, the baby's life support system became compromised and the life of the mother was in jeopardy. It would have been dangerous enough in hospital, but all Abby and Mac had was some morphine and basic equipment. It wasn't good. Abby's heart jumped to her throat.

Mac paused by the doorway and hunkered down so that he was at eye level with the boy. He placed a hand on the child's shoulder.

'What's your name, son?'

'Tim.'

'It's going to be all right, Tim, I promise. Now, if you could take us to your mum, we'll look after her.'

Whatever Tim saw in Mac's eyes seemed to reassure him. He nodded and led them inside the farmhouse and into a bedroom. On the bed, a woman lay writhing with pain. She was pale and her eyes were stretched wide with fear.

Abby and Mac rushed to her side.

'Jenny, isn't it?' Mac said as he laid the medical case on the floor. 'I'm Dr MacNeil and this is Abby Stevens. We're going to do everything we can to look after you and your baby.'

Abby felt Jenny's pulse.

'Over one hundred and thready,' she told Mac as she unwrapped the stethoscope from around her neck.

'How long have you been bleeding? And when did the contractions start?' Mac asked.

'I just started bleeding a few minutes ago. The contractions started about an hour ago. I phoned the hospital and they said they would get an ambulance.' Jenny reached out a hand and squeezed Abby's fingers hard. 'You have to save my baby. Please. You've got to help us.'

'We are going to do everything possible,' Abby replied with what she hoped was a confident smile.

She checked Jenny's blood pressure. As expected, it was low. Jenny was already bleeding heavily.

'I'm just going to give you some fluids through a needle in your vein,' Mac explained as he swabbed a patch of skin near Jenny's elbow. 'Then we're going to get you onto a stretcher and into the air ambulance, okay?'

'What about Tim? I can't leave him here by himself. My husband isn't due back until tomorrow morning.'

'Is there a neighbour we could call for you?'

Jenny shook her head. 'We only moved here a couple of months ago. I don't know anyone yet. I've been so busy getting ready for the new baby.'

'In that case, Tim can come in the helicopter with us. How about it, Tim?' Mac turned to the little boy who had remained by the door, taking everything in with wide eyes.

'Wicked,' he said. Now adults were taking control, the colour had returned to his face.

Mac finished setting up the drip.

'Okay, Jenny. The helicopter's just outside waiting to take you to hospital. We're going to get you on board as quickly as we can.'

Jenny clutched her stomach as another contraction took hold. 'Just get me to the hospital,' she said through gritted teeth. Then she forced a smile and turned to her son. 'Tim will help, won't you, love?'

Tim's terror had disappeared. Whether it was because they were there helping his mother or whether it was the excitement of the helicopter ride, Abby didn't know or care. All that mattered was that the boy was calm. It would help Jenny and give them one less thing to worry about.

Abby draped a blanket round her patient before strapping her into the stretcher. As they carried her outside, Abby tried not to wince when a contraction gripped the mother and she squeezed Abby's fingers with ferocious strength.

Please let her hang in there, Abby prayed silently. At least until they got her to hospital. She slid a glance at Mac. Nothing in his demeanour indicated that at any time they could be dealing with a life-and-death scenario. Was he really as calm as he appeared?

Inside the helicopter they attached Jenny to the on-board monitoring equipment and pumped fluids into her. Abby checked the fetal heartbeat again. So far so good.

As soon as they had Jenny settled and the helicopter was heading towards St Piran's, Mac raised his thumb to Tim. Greg had given the boy a helmet and earmuffs to deaden the noise.

Tim returned the salute, unable to hide his excitement.

Abby slid a glance at Mac as he leaned over Jenny. He puzzled her. Everything about him contradicted the image of him she had held in her head for the last twelve years. Whenever she'd thought about him, she'd imagined an ageing Lothario chatting up young women on the beach under the pretext of teaching them how to windsurf, not this caring and utterly professional doctor.

Even if it was obvious from his behaviour when they'd met as well as Lucy's comments that he still was a blatant flirt she liked the way he had taken the time to reassure Tim.

Her thoughts were interrupted as the helicopter touched down on the hospital landing pad. Abby breathed a deep sigh of relief. They had made it!

'Stick close to me,' Mac said to Tim after removing the young lad's helmet.

The helicopter's rotors hadn't even stopped when the hospital staff were there to take charge of Jenny. The transfer was quick. Mac and Abby updated the hospital staff as they ran next to the trolley with Tim following closely behind.

'Thanks, guys. We'll take it from here,' the doctor Mac had addressed as Dr Gibson said.

They watched as Jenny disappeared from view.

'C'mon, Tim. Why don't we get you a drink or something?' Abby offered, knowing that now the excitement of the helicopter journey was over the boy would start fretting again. 'And in the meantime we can try and get your dad on the phone and either me or Dr MacNeil here will speak to him. How does that sound?'

'Sounds okay. When can I see Mum?'

'Not for a little while,' Abby said. 'But while Dr MacNeil is speaking to your father, I'll find somewhere where you can wait.'

Tim's face crumpled. 'I don't want to stay on my own. I want my dad.'

Abby felt terrible for the little boy. If something happened to her, she'd hate for Emma to be left alone. But what could they do? They had to get back to the air ambulance base. There could be another call at any time.

But Mac seemed to have his own ideas. 'Tell you what,' he said. 'When I speak to your dad, I'll suggest you come back with Abby and me to the air ambulance headquarters. How about it? You could have a look around see all the stuff we use. We have some cool things we can do with our computers. I'll let the staff here know where we are and as soon as they have any news about your mum they can let us know. What do you say?'

Tim's face brightened. 'Could I? No one will mind? I promise I won't get in the way.'

Once more, Abby was pleasantly surprised. Mac could easily have left the child here. After all they had done their job and Tim wasn't their responsibility. She really had underestimated him. Nothing about him made sense. Her head was beginning to ache. Right now she would have given anything for some time on her own to think, but she had promised Tim a drink while they waited for Mac to speak to his father and do the handover.

Spotting a vending machine against the wall inside the A & E department, Abby scrabbled in her pocket for some change and fed it into the slot. To no avail—the wretched machine stubbornly refused to part with its goods. Banging with the flat of her hand against the side had no effect either.

'Here, let me help.' A woman who looked as if she had stepped out of a magazine came across. She fiddled with the machine and a can rolled out.

'It just takes a certain knack.' She held out a manicured hand. 'You must be new. I'm Rebecca O'Hara, my husband Josh is one of the A & E consultants.'

'Abby Stevens. First day with the Air Ambulance Service.'

'Pleased to meet you, Abby. Where are you from? I can tell by your accent that you're not from here.'

'I've been living in London for the last few years.'

'London?' Rebecca looked wistful. 'Don't you miss it?'

'I love it here,' Abby said honestly. She glanced across the room to where an anxious Tim was waiting for her. Although she had the distinct impression Rebecca wanted to chat, Abby didn't like to leave the boy any longer than she had to.

Just then Mac appeared. 'Oh, hello, Rebecca.' He smiled. 'If you're waiting to see Josh, I'm afraid he's up to his neck with patients at the moment.'

Rebecca looked dejected. 'I'll have a cup of coffee with the nurses while I'm waiting.'

She turned back to Abby. 'Lovely to meet you.

Perhaps we could have a coffee some time?' And then with a flutter of slim fingers she headed towards the staffroom.

Back at base, no one seemed particularly surprised to see Tim. Mac gave him the promised tour after which he settled Tim in front of the computers and started explaining how the system worked.

A little while later, Dr Gibson phoned to say that they had sectioned Jenny and although she had lost a great deal of blood, she and her new baby son were going to be fine. Tim was ecstatic about having a brother, but as it was going to be a couple of hours before Jenny would come around properly from the anaesthetic, they decided to keep him with them a bit longer. Tim's father was on his way to the hospital.

'I'll drop Tim back at the hospital later,' Mac said to Abby. 'I'm due to do some teaching there this afternoon.'

Abby raised an eyebrow.

'I keep my hand in at the hospital when we're not busy. It helps keep me up to date and it only takes me a couple of minutes to get back here if we get a call-out.' He smiled. 'You don't fancy a drink later, by any chance? I can tell you all about Penhally.' His expression was teasing, his eyes glinting.

Abby was horrified to feel a tingle run down her spine. Damn it! Why did she have to find him so damn sexy? Even sexier and better looking than twelve years ago. And the fact that he had a caring side made him all the more attractive. What was she thinking? There was no way she could be attracted to her dead sister's ex-lover; it was too weird. What was more, she had to remember that Mac was the type of man for whom flirting was as natural as breathing. It didn't mean anything. Wasn't the way he'd treated Sara evidence of that?

He was looking at her, waiting for her reply, certain she would say yes. He was so supremely confident she would love to turn him down. And she would have, if it wasn't for Emma. Her antennae, honed by years of being let down by men just like him, were on red alert. Of all the men in all the world, why did she have to be working with him?

Despite every nerve cell in her brain telling her to keep her distance from this man, for her daughter's sake, she needed to learn more about him. Emma was going to a friend's after school and wouldn't be home until seven. Abby made up her mind.

'I'll tell you what,' she said. 'I like to go for a walk after work. You can join me if you want.' She shrugged. 'It's up to you.' Smiling to herself as she saw the look of surprise in his eyes, she whirled on her heel, ignoring the feeling that two blue eyes were watching her speculatively.

Mac watched Abby's retreating back until she was out of sight. He would have bet a hundred bucks she had been about to turn him down, and her acceptance had taken him by surprise. Not that a walk was what he had in mind and not that he would have let one refusal put him off. In fact, it would have heightened the excitement of the chase. He tried to ignore the unpleasant feeling lurking somewhere deep down that felt uncomfortably like shame. Should he really be going after Abby? Although she intrigued and excited him, there was a certain wariness about her that suggested she had been hurt before, perhaps badly. And then there was the odd way she had kept looking at him during the callout. For someone as experienced as she was supposed to be there was an edginess about her that, while not quite alarming him, concerned him a little.

There was something else about Abby that was niggling him. He could have sworn he had met her before, but he had to be mistaken. He might have been with a lot of women in his life, but he would never have forgotten someone like her.

What was her story anyway? Not that it really mattered. He liked women, enjoyed their company and had a lot of respect for them, but he had no intention of having a long-term relationship with one. Once they made demands on him, he couldn't help but lose interest. But he was getting way ahead of himself. This was simply a walk with a colleague, albeit a beautiful one. What was the harm in that? Nevertheless, however much he tried to dismiss the feeling of unease, he couldn't quite shake it. A sixth sense he had relied on all his life was telling him that something extraordinary had arrived in the form of Abby Stevens and he wasn't sure he liked the feeling one little bit.

CHAPTER THREE

MAC was leaning against the side of a four-by-four, looking relaxed, when Abby eventually emerged at the end of her shift. After changing out of her jumpsuit, she had taken a few moments to put on some lipstick and brush her hair. She told herself that she wasn't preening herself for Mac, it was simply that she needed the confidence of make-up as well as the time to get her thumping heart rate under control. But she knew deep down that wasn't the whole truth. Wasn't there just a tiny part of her that liked it that he had made it clear he was attracted to her? She dismissed the thought immediately. This wasn't about her. It was about Emma.

Mac was wearing a pair of faded jeans and a white T-shirt under a well-worn leather jacket. His teeth flashed in a wide grin when he saw her. Surely it was anxiety over what she had to tell him that made her stomach flip?

He opened the passenger door of the Jeep with a flourish.

'There's an interesting cliff walk about ten minutes' drive from here. There's a fantastic fish restaurant nearby. We could have something to eat after our walk and I'll drive you back here so you can collect your car.' He paused. 'Unless you want to leave your car at your house? I could follow you home and we could leave from there. Where is it you live, anyway?'

Something in the way his eyes were glittering made Abby wonder if he was imagining an ending to the evening that included him and her in bed together. Little did he know there was a greater chance of hell freezing over.

'I'm renting a cottage in Penhally Bay while I look around for a place to buy. But I'd rather follow you in my own car. And as for supper…' she shook her head '…sorry, I have other plans.' A walk was one thing, a meal *à deux* quite another.

Mac frowned and Abby felt a small stab of triumph. He was clearly a man who was used to getting his own way. Well, he'd find out soon enough that she liked having her way, too.

She followed his four-by-four, uncomfortably aware of the anxiety that was coiling in her chest. He had no idea about the bombshell she was soon going to be dropping into his life. For a second she felt sorry for him, but only for a second. Emma was the only person who mattered in this whole sorry mess.

The sun was slipping lower, streaking the sky with gold, but it would be light for another hour or two. There was still a hint of warmth in the air, and the earlier wind had subsided. It was a perfect October evening, with just a hint of summer still.

The hordes of tourists had long since left and there was only one other car in the car park as they parked their cars side by side.

'The walk I had in mind is a couple of miles each way,' Mac said. 'That's not too far for you, is it?'

'I like walking,' Abby said. 'As long as I'm home for seven.'

She had to walk rapidly to keep up with Mac's long strides. He glanced down and checked his pace so it matched hers.

'How are Jenny and the baby doing?' she asked. As promised, Mac had taken Tim back to the hospital where his father had been waiting for him.

Mac frowned. 'Last I knew, mother and baby were doing fine. Why, did you hear something?' There was no mistaking the concern in his eyes.

'No, I haven't heard anything.' Abby said. 'I just thought you might have popped in to see her when you were at the hospital.'

Mac looked puzzled. 'Why would I do that?'

'Don't you follow up on your patients? Aren't you curious to know how everything turned out?'

He shook his head. 'I treat them, look after them as best I can, then let the hospital staff do their bit. All I care about is giving the best treatment I am capable of. I don't see the point in getting too involved with patients. We have to know when to let go, so we can move on to the next one.'

Abby was dismayed. Once again it seemed she had got this man wrong. Could he really be as disinterested in his patients as he seemed? Abby couldn't imagine not following up on her patients. Most of the time, out there on a rescue, she formed a strong bond with the people whose lives depended on her. It was part of who she was.

'So tell me, what brings you here, to Cornwall and Penhally Bay in particular?' Mac changed the subject. 'Someone mentioned you'd been working with the London ambulance service for the last eleven years. What happened? Did you get tired of the big city?'

Anxiety raced along her spine. It was the perfect

moment to tell him about Emma, but she wasn't ready. Not yet. Not until she knew more about him. Once she told him there would be no going back.

'My daughter needed a change of air,' Abby said evasively. 'And I needed a change of scenery.'

'You have a daughter? I didn't know.' He sounded surprised...and regretful.

Abby suspected he wouldn't have been so keen to ask her out if he'd known she had a child. Most of the men she had dated in the past had reacted the same way. They all backed off when she told them and if they didn't, her refusal to put them before Emma usually made them give up on her sooner or later. And that was fine. She didn't need or want a man in her life who couldn't accept Emma. Not even this one. *Particularly* not this one.

He flicked his eyes to her left hand again. 'You don't wear a ring so I'm guessing you're not married.'

'I'm a single mum.' Let him make of that what he would. He would know the truth soon enough. First she had some questions of her own.

'What about you? I assume you're not married?'

'Nope. Not the marrying kind, I guess.'

'Children?' Abby held her breath as she waited for his reply.

'No, none of them either. Not the father kind.'

Little did he know.

'How long have you worked for the air ambulance?' Abby asked.

'Two years. I completed my specialist training in anaesthesia, then I did a course in medical emergency retrieval in Glasgow. But unfortunately the surfing conditions aren't great there, so when I found they were looking for a rescue medic here, I jumped at the chance. It means I can kite board when I'm not working.'

So his sport was as important as his job. Maybe more so. Abby was disappointed. Minute by minute she was having to revise her opinion of the man who was Emma's father.

'Although I can tell you're Scottish from your accent, it doesn't sound very Glaswegian,' Abby probed. The more she knew about this man, the better.

'I was brought up on Tiree. It's an island off the west coast of Scotland. I lived there until I went to medical school in Glasgow when I was eighteen. I don't go back to Tiree very often.' His mouth tightened and as Abby glanced at him she could have sworn she saw anger behind his eyes, but it disappeared so quickly she couldn't be sure. Did Mac have secrets of his own?

She was about to question him further when he stopped in his tracks. She followed his gaze to see what had caught his attention. To their left, close to the edge, a man was pacing frantically up and down, shouting a boy's name.

'Something's wrong,' Mac said. 'I'm going to take a look-see.'

As Mac called out, the man turned to them, relief evident under his panic.

'It's my son,' he said. 'I can't find him! One minute he was here, and then the next he was gone. I only meant to close my eyes for a minute, but I must have dropped off. You've got to help me find him. He's only eight.' The man's eyes were darting around while he was speaking.

Mac placed a hand on his shoulder. 'Stay calm and tell me everything. What's your name?'

'Dave. My son's called Luke.'

'Where did you last see Luke?'

'He was over there.' The man pointed behind him.

'He wanted to go down to the beach but I told him there was no path. I said I'd take him there tomorrow. Oh, my God. What if he tried to go down by himself and fell?'

'Have you phoned for help?'

'No, I haven't had time. I've been too busy looking for him.'

Mac's eyes raked the side of the cliff. Something caught his attention and he stopped and sucked in a breath. Abby followed his gaze. Near the edge, a piece of the cliff had broken away. From the look of it, it had only happened very recently. Seeing the troubled look in Mac's eyes, she knew he was thinking the same thing. There was a good chance the boy had got too close to the edge and slipped over. If they were right and the boy had fallen, he could be badly hurt, or worse.

'Abby. Phone 999 and get them to alert the coastguard and the rescue services. Dave, I'm just going to have a look over this cliff and see if I can see him. You stay back, okay?'

Abby touched Dave's shoulder reassuringly as she used her mobile. It was still possible the boy had wandered off and was nowhere near the cliff but they couldn't take the chance.

Mac walked close to the cliff then dropped to his stomach to peer over the edge. 'I think I can see him,' he called. 'Is he wearing a red jacket?'

Luke's father rushed forward. Mac jumped to his feet and barred his way.

'You have to stay back,' Mac warned. 'The edge here is already unstable. If you come any closer you could slip or a bit of the cliff could crumble and fall on your son.

'I'm going to climb down there and see how he is, okay?' Mac added quietly.

'Shouldn't we wait for the rescue services?' Abby said. 'The operator said they shouldn't be more than ten minutes. If you go down there, you could fall, too.'

Mac dug in his pocket and pulled out his car keys. He tossed them to Dave. 'Dave, go back to the car park. My car is the Jeep. In the boot you'll find a red medical case, a rope and a yellow jacket. Could you fetch them?'

Dave hesitated and Mac gave him a gentle push. 'Go! It's the best way to help Luke. Be as quick as you can.'

As soon as Dave had set off at a run, Mac turned back to Abby. 'We don't have time to wait for help.' While he was talking he had removed his jacket. 'I'm going to go down. When Dave returns I might need you to lower my medical bag on the end of the rope. Okay?' He moved towards the cliff.

'Shouldn't you at least wait for the rope?' If Mac fell they would have two victims to rescue. Even in her anxiety, the irony wasn't completely lost on her. She had just found Emma's father. If he fell now, Emma might never get to know him.

Mac turned around and grinned. 'Hey, I was brought up near cliffs. Never met one yet I couldn't beat. I'll be okay. As soon as you hear the rescue 'copter, let off a flare. Keep Dave occupied by telling him to search for a good place for the helicopter to land.'

Before she could protest further, he disappeared over the edge.

Abby's heart banged against her ribs. What was Mac thinking? Although if it had been Emma down there, she would have gone herself. Fear of heights or not.

She tiptoed over to the edge, following Mac's earlier

example, and lay flat on her stomach and peered over. Although Mac was picking his way carefully down the cliff he was moving faster than she would have thought was safe. From this vantage point she could see that although the cliff was steep, it didn't fall away as sharply as she'd thought. Relief swept through her. Perhaps Luke had a chance.

As Dave returned with the bag, rope and Mac's fluorescent jacket she became aware of a whooping sound in the distance. Shielding her eyes against the sinking sun, she could just about make out the large yellow shape of a Sea King helicopter. Thank God! They would have proper equipment and hopefully a way to get both Mac and Luke up.

'Come on.' She jumped up and shouted across to Dave. 'We need to find a decent landing place to direct the pilot to land.'

'How is my son? Could you see him? Is he okay?'

Abby moved towards open ground and yelled back over her shoulder. 'Mac will be with him in a few minutes. He's a doctor. He'll do everything he can to help Luke.'

Without waiting to see whether Dave was following or not, she raced over to the flat piece of ground. It was just about big enough for the helicopter to land and thankfully the previous days' rain had run away, leaving it solid underfoot.

Abby waved Mac's jacket and immediately the helicopter headed in their direction. Dave was standing behind her, looking lost and terrified. She summoned up a smile. 'I promise you, your son is in good hands.' And she believed it. 'Stay back until they land, then tell them everything. Okay? I'm going to lower the medical bag down to Mac.'

She ran back to the cliff edge and dropped on to her front again. Mac was at the bottom now and kneeling next to the prone figure of the boy. At least he had made it down in one piece. But Mac couldn't risk moving the child on his own. If Luke had survived the fall, there was every chance he had serious neck and head injuries and any movement could mean the difference between a full recovery and life in a wheelchair.

Mac glanced up and gave her a thumbs-up. Luke must still be alive. She tied the medical bag to the rope and lowered it down but it snagged on the jagged rock face. The incline may have helped Mac reach the boy, but it was hampering her efforts to get the bag down to him. Almost crying with frustration, she was only vaguely aware of a hand touching her shoulder. She looked up into calm green eyes of a crew member from the helicopter.

'Miss, you have to stand away from the edge.' Before she could protest, the man took her arm and raised her to her feet. 'We'll take it from here.'

'Mac—Dr MacNeil—is down there with the boy. Mac's a doctor with the air ambulance. He needs his bag.'

'Mac, as in Daredevil Mac?' A broad smile spread across the man's craggy face. 'Well I'll be bug—blown. We know him well, and if he's onto it, everything will be A-okay. Don't worry, I'll get the bag down to him.'

Pulling the case back up, the man, whose name badge said Roberts, took it and ran back to the helicopter. Seconds later the Sea King took off again.

Abby joined Dave, knowing that for the time being there was little she or the anxious father could do. She hooked her arm in his as they watched the helicopter hover over the cliff. A couple of tense minutes passed before a figure, clutching a stretcher and the medical bag, was lowered from the side of the helicopter. Abby's heart thudded painfully. In many ways she would have preferred to be down there helping. This waiting was worse than anything.

Minutes crawled like hours. Then suddenly the crewman came back into view. He was holding onto the stretcher, which now contained a figure. Immediately after the winchman and the stretcher were pulled on board, the helicopter lowered the rope again and after a few moments Mac appeared above the top of the cliff. He, too, was pulled into the waiting Sea King.

Instead of flying off, the helicopter landed again. Abby grabbed Dave's hand and ran towards it. Roberts had barely pulled her and Dave in before the helicopter banked away. Roberts passed her a helmet with a radio attached.

With a brief word to Dave to stay where he was, Abby hurried over to Mac, who was bent over the stretcher.

'He has a compound fracture of the femur. I can't rule out internal injuries and of course we have to suspect head and spinal injuries. I've given him IV morphine for the pain.'

Mac attached his patient to the pulse oximeter while Abby checked Luke's vital signs.

Although Luke's blood pressure was low and his pulse elevated, and he wasn't out of the woods yet, he was a very lucky boy. His leg would take time to heal and would have hurt like crazy before the morphine took effect, but as long as he didn't have internal injuries he'd probably be able to leave hospital in a week or two. Abby shuddered when she thought what might have happened if she and Mac hadn't come across Dave when they had. She was even more confused about Mac than ever. He had risked his life for Luke, he had been thoughtful with Tim, yet he had made it clear that he didn't believe in getting involved with patients. Which one was the real Mac?

Luke tried to sit up, but Abby pushed him gently back down.

'Dad?' he asked. 'Where's my dad?'

Abby beckoned to Dave to come forward. Anything to help the child stay calm was good.

'He's right here,' Abby said gently. She moved away slightly so Luke could see his father. Both father and son started to cry. 'Dave, you need to move away again so we can work on your son, okay? Try not to worry, I'm sure he's going to be okay.'

When they touched down at St Piran's the staff from A & E were waiting for them.

'Status update?' the A & E consultant, bearing the name badge Dr Josh O'Hara, asked. Abby had only the briefest impression of dark hair and deep blue eyes before Luke was rushed inside.

Abby, her part in the drama over, went in search of Dave. He would be desperate for news of his injured child. She found him sitting outside Resus, his head in his hands.

She tapped him gently on his shoulder. 'Dave.'

He looked at her with red-rimmed eyes. He tried to speak, but couldn't. He shook his head, almost as if he were too scared to ask after his son.

'How is he?' he managed after clearing his throat.

Abby sat next to him and took his hand in hers.

'I think he'll be fine, Dave. It was good we found him when we did, and that we were able to start giving him medical treatment straight away. All that will make a big difference to his recovery.'

They sat in silence for a moment. 'Is there anyone I can call for you? Luke's mother? She'll need to know he's in hospital.'

Dave took a deep shuddering breath. 'She's dead.' He buried his face in his hands. 'She died from breast cancer six months ago.'

'I'm so sorry,' Abby said.

Dave's eyes were bleak. 'She'd never forgive me if I let something happen to our child. I promised her I'd look after him and I fell asleep. What kind of father am I?'

'You're human. It can be difficult, bringing up a child on your own. You can't watch them all the time.'

Dave raked a hand through his hair. 'But I fell asleep! I've been working overtime so I could afford to take Luke away on holiday. So he and I could spend more time together. He needs something to cheer him up. The loss of his mum was a terrible blow. To both of us.' Abby was only dimly aware of Mac coming to stand next to them. 'And I could have lost him, too.'

'You've not lost him,' Mac said quietly. 'He's got to go to Theatre to get his leg pinned where it was broken, but he's going to be fine.'

'He's going to be okay?' Dave said almost as if he didn't dare allow himself to believe what Mac was telling him. The relief in Dave's eyes brought a lump to Abby's throat.

'Yes, he is. I promise you,' Mac said firmly. 'You can see him for a few moments before he goes to Theatre, if you like.'

Dave sprang to his feet. He clasped Mac's hands in his. 'How can I ever thank you? I know you put your own life in danger and I'll never forget you for that.

Either of you.' Without giving them a chance to reply, he rushed away to see his son.

'Another satisfied customer,' Mac said wryly. 'Perhaps he'll take better care of his son after this.' He rubbed a hand across his chin. 'What the hell was he thinking? Having a nap while his eight-year-old played near a dangerous cliff. Some people just shouldn't have children.'

Abby rounded on him. 'He's doing the best he can. Do you know he only fell asleep because he's been working all hours to give his son a holiday? Luke's mother died recently and Dave has been doing the best he can to care for him. Being a single parent isn't easy. We all make mistakes. It's just by the grace of God, most of the time, things turn out all right.' What the hell did Mac know about being a parent, the demands, the worry?

Mac held up his hands as if to ward off her words. He looked stunned and contrite. 'Hey, I had no idea.'

'You shouldn't be so quick to judge, Mac. As the saying goes, you don't know what a person's life is like until you've walked in their shoes.'

Mac narrowed his eyes, his expression unreadable. 'I have no intention of ever walking in his shoes, as you put it.' The clouds cleared from his face. 'But I didn't know his circumstances,' he said. 'If I had, I wouldn't have been so quick to make assumptions.' He smiled ruefully. 'I stand corrected.'

Their eyes locked and Abby's heart somersaulted. She had the strangest feeling that he knew every thought that was rattling around her confused brain. Dismayed, she pulled her eyes away from his searching gaze and glanced at her watch. She had to get back for Emma, but her car was still miles away where she had left it when she and Mac had set out on their walk.

Mac caught her look of alarm. 'What is it?'

'I need to get home,' she said. 'Like now. But my car's on the other side of Penhally, still in the car park.'

'Mine, too,' Mac glanced up as Josh emerged from Resus.

'Know where I could borrow a car, mate?' Mac asked.

Josh dug in his pocket and fished out a set of keys. He tossed them at Mac, who caught them.

'Take mine,' Josh said. 'Just make sure you bring it back in one piece.'

'Hey.' Mac pretended to look offended. 'Don't I always?'

Josh raised an eyebrow. 'You know it's only a matter of time if you continue to drive like the devil.'

'I only drive fast when I'm on my own. And when the road allows. Your car will be perfectly safe.' Mac turned to Abby. 'I'll drop you off at your house then collect your car.'

Abby wasn't at all sure she wanted to be in a car with Mac after hearing Josh's comments, but she did have to get home. Emma was too young to be left on her own, even for a short while. 'What about yours?' Abby protested.

'Don't worry about mine. It's not a problem. I can get it any time.'

Inside Josh's car, Abby glanced at her watch again. She should make it before Emma. With a bit of luck.

'You did a brave thing back there,' she said as they drove down the narrow lanes in the direction of Penhally Bay.

Mac grinned at her and her pulse scrambled. He was having the strangest effect on her. As if she didn't have enough to contend with. Leftover adrenaline, she told herself.

'As I said before, it was a piece of cake. Where is your house?'

Abby gave him the address and he nodded. 'I think I know where you are.'

'But don't you think you were a little reckless?' Abby persisted. 'You could have been killed, or fallen and then we would have had two bodies to rescue.' *And Emma wouldn't have a father, suitable or unsuitable.*

Mac slid her a glance. 'Where's the fun in life if you can't take risks?' he said. 'You might as well be dead if you don't. And, anyway, I knew I could climb down to him. Believe me, it wasn't nearly as dangerous as it looked. At least, not for me. Free climbing is one of my hobbies.'

Abby frowned. She didn't like the sound of this free climbing, whatever it was.

'Which means what exactly?'

'It's a form of climbing where you don't use ropes. Great fun.'

Oh, dear Lord. Emma's father was an adrenaline junkie who didn't seem to care whether he lived or died. Could it get any worse?

'Oh, and by the way,' Mac said, following her pointed finger, as he pulled up in front of the small two-up, two-down where she and Emma lived. 'You owe me a date. And one thing you should know about me is that I always collect my debts.' His diamond-coloured eyes locked onto hers and once again Abby had the strangest feeling he could see into her soul.

The blood rushed to her cheeks. It was as if someone had lit a fire just below her skin and it was smouldering away. Any minute now she'd go up in a puff of smoke.

She was out of the car almost before it had come to a complete stop. So far none of this was going the way she'd planned.

Shortly after Mac left, Emma came running into the cottage and flung herself down on the sofa. She beamed happily at Abby.

'Hey. I gather you had a good time?' Abby asked.

'It was great. A few of the other girls came over and we had the coolest time trying on each other's clothes and make-up. Not one of them asked me anything about my dad. I don't think they care at all.'

'Those girls in your other school were the exception, Emma. They just had to make themselves feel good by putting you down.' She ruffled her daughter's hair. Whatever happened with Mac, they had made the right decision coming here. In the last few weeks Emma had changed back from the subdued, under-confident girl she had become in London to the lively fun-loving kid she had always been before that.

Emma jumped up from the sofa and hugged Abby fiercely. 'You're the best mum in the world,' she said.

Abby's heart twisted. All she had ever wanted was to give Emma the security and love she and Sara had never experienced. There was nothing she wouldn't do for Emma. Not even risk losing her to her father. If that father could make her happy. What she was not prepared to do now that Emma was just getting back to her bright usual self was risk her daughter being rejected. Abby knew only too well how that felt.

'Sara loved you as much as I do. You'll never forget that, will you?'

'I know. You tell me that almost every day.' Emma looked sad for a moment. 'I really wish I could have known her.' But in the way kids did, her face brightened almost immediately. 'At least I have you to tell me all the stories about her. I love hearing the ones about how you both kept getting into trouble. They make me laugh.'

'Yes, but, remember, I only tell you some of these stories as a warning about how easily you can get into trouble.' Abby was stricken. What if Emma tried to copy some of the pranks she and Sara had got up to? It didn't bear thinking about.

Emma grinned. 'You are so easy to tease, Mum. I get you every time.'

'Why don't you have your shower while I get supper ready?' Abby suggested. 'Then afterwards there's a movie on TV we can watch together.' Mac would be back any minute with her car, and she wasn't ready for child and father to meet.

And that wasn't the only thing she wasn't prepared for, Abby admitted to herself as she set about preparing supper. She hadn't expected to find herself reacting to him the way she did. The way her heart kept misbehaving every time he was around wasn't just down to her anxiety about Emma and was an unwelcome complication in a situation that was already complicated enough. Damn it, why did he have to be so infuriatingly gorgeous?

As she'd hoped. Emma was still in the shower when Mac arrived with her car. In her haste to have him gone before Emma came downstairs, she practically grabbed her car keys from his hand. All this emotional turmoil was exhausting. She knew she couldn't keep father and daughter apart for ever. Sooner or later, she would have to tell them the truth.

CHAPTER FOUR

BACK at work, Mac didn't mention another date. Abby wasn't sure if she was relieved or offended. For her second shift, she worked with Lucy, attending a car accident as well as a child with breathing difficulties. Although she enjoyed working with Lucy, she had to admit she was disappointed that she wouldn't always be working with Mac. She told herself it was simply because she was trying to figure him out and nothing to do with the fact she felt alert, more alive somehow, when he was around.

Every now and again she would look up to find his eyes on her. He would grin as if he'd caught her out and she would look away quickly, terrified in case he noticed the blush stealing up her cheeks.

'What do you say we go for a walk down on the beach?' Abby suggested to Emma one day after work. Although it was after five, it was unseasonably warm for October.

'Great. Can I go swimming?' Emma asked, and before Abby could reply she was off upstairs to her small bedroom. Emma had to be constantly on the go.

Abby fetched her own costume from the bedroom opposite Emma's. She slipped into her bikini before pulling on a long, silky cardigan to cover her until they got to the beach. Their rented home was tiny, having once been a fisherman's cottage. It had a sitting room and a small kitchen downstairs and two bedrooms upstairs with a small bathroom separating them. Abby would have preferred something bigger, but her salary as a paramedic didn't stretch very far. After rent and food, anything left over went on clothes and outings for Emma. Sometimes it was a struggle to make ends meet, but if the alternative had been not having Emma in her life, Abby knew it was no contest. Over the years she had scrimped and saved until she had some savings in the bank. Enough to put a deposit down on a small house when they found the right place. At least here in Penhally they had a chance of getting on the housing ladder. In London, it had been impossible.

'I'm ready. Let's go,' Emma called to Abby.

The beach was a ten-minute walk from their house. Although the tourists were away, the sun still warmed the air and there were plenty of locals making the most of the last few warm evenings.

As they walked, Emma asked Abby about her job.

'I love it. The rest of the team seem really nice. I went on my first rescue on Monday with one of the doctors. We managed to get a woman to hospital so her baby could be born safely. We also had to rescue a boy who had fallen down a cliff. Being here has different dangers from those in London. Ones that you might not even think about. So, please, Emma, you need to be very careful when you're out with your friends.'

'You worry too much, Mum. Nothing will happen to me.'

Abby smiled at her daughter. 'I know it won't. And I know I'm a worry wart. But just promise me you'll always be careful.' She couldn't bear it if anything happened to her.

'I might be a pilot when I grow up,' Emma said, dismissing Abby's fears. 'I think I would like flying off to help people in trouble.'

Trust Emma to be drawn to that kind of career. The little girl loved nothing better than taking on anything that was exciting. It struck Abby that she shared at least one trait with Mac. The worst possible, in Abby's opinion. How many more would there be? 'You can be anything you like, darling. As long as you stick at school and do your best.'

Emma stuck out her tongue. 'C'mon, Mum. I'll race you to the sea.' And with that she was off, long legs flying across the sand and her blonde hair streaming behind her. Abby laughed and raced behind her daughter, her heart feeling as light as it had for as long as she could remember.

The shore was busy with people either walking their dogs, playing ball games or paddling. To one side, in an area cordoned off, were the surfers, windsurfers and kite boarders. Abby had watched them once or twice before, impressed at their skill.

The wind down at the shore was gustier than it had been at the cottage and the surfers were taking full advantage of the substantial waves. Further out, where the waves were even bigger, was a kite boarder. Abby and Emma stopped paddling to watch as the boarder let his parachute pull him into the air. There was a collective gasp from other people who had stopped to watch as he somersaulted in the air before landing perfectly on the water. He caught the wind in his parachute to propel him across the water, faster than Abby had ever seen anyone move without the use of an engine. Just as she thought he was going to crash onto the beach, he flipped in the air again, this time landing so he faced in the opposite direction. Abby had never seen anything quite as graceful before. Although the figure was tall, well over six feet, his movements in the air were almost balletic.

'I want to learn how to do that,' Emma said, her eyes wide with admiration. 'It looks so cool.'

Over my dead body, Abby thought grimly. It was far too dangerous. But she didn't say anything. Experience of her headstrong daughter had taught her that the more Emma was told not to do something, the more she wanted to do it. In that way she was very like Sara.

'I think you have to learn to surf or windsurf first, before you can move onto something like that,' Abby said mildly. With a bit of luck it would take Emma years to master the basics. And by that time she would have forgotten her interest in kite surfing.

The kite surfer was racing back towards the shore. When he was only a metre or so away, he turned his board sideways and jumped off. He seemed to have given up for the day.

As he walked up the beach, Abby's breath caught in her throat. It was Mac. He shook the water from his hair before peeling his suit down to his waist. Abby sucked in her breath. His chest was as muscled as she'd remembered, the six pack of his abdomen even more defined than twelve years earlier. All at once a memory of the first time she had seen him came flooding back.

It had been the first full day of their holiday on Mykonos and Abby had been looking forward to relaxing in the sun with Sara. The last few years had been tough. Since their mother had more or less evicted them from the family home, Sara's behaviour had become wilder and wilder. Although Abby had trained as a paramedic, Sara had not found a job she'd wanted to do for more than a few weeks. More interested in partying than working, Sara had lost more than one job for failing to turn up for work after a late night. Abby had hoped that their holiday would give her a chance to talk to Sara and make her see that sooner or later she had to settle down.

As they'd made themselves comfortable on their sun-loungers, Abby's attention had been caught by a tall windsurfing instructor who had been giving lessons to a group of beginners on the beach close by. His height alone would have caught her attention, but his tanned and toned physique had made him stand out like some Greek god. His sun-bleached hair had reflected the sun and when he'd grinned, which had been often, his eyes glinted. Abby had never seen anyone whose presence had been so immediate before and her stomach had flipped. He must have felt the intensity of her gaze as he'd looked up from what he was doing and, catching her eye, had winked with a wide smile. Abby had blushed and dipped her head.

Sara had noticed and followed her gaze to where Mac had returned his attention to his class and had been demonstrating how to move the sail on the board in order to catch the wind.

'Now, that's what I call hot,' Sara said appreciatively. 'I think I've just signed up to windsurfing classes.' Not having a shy bone in her body, Sara sauntered over to join the group, and that was more or less the last Abby saw of her for the rest of the holiday. Instead of the girly chats Abby had envisaged, from that moment Sara spent every spare minute with Mac, leaving Abby to amuse herself.

* * *

Abby was forced back to the present as Mac noticed them standing on the beach and walked up to them. He smiled widely.

'Fancy meeting you here,' he said to Abby. His eyes glinted as they lingered on her bikini-clad figure and Abby resisted the impulse to wrap her arms around her body to shield herself from his appreciative gaze.

'We were watching you out there. Pretty impressive.' Abby's heart was in her throat. This wasn't how she'd planned father and daughter would meet.

'Yes. It was really wicked,' Emma piped up.

He turned his gaze to Emma and raised a quizzical eyebrow at Abby.

'This is my daughter, Emma. Emma, this is Dr William MacNeil, my colleague.' *And your father.*

'I'm pleased to meet you, Emma,' Mac said with a tip of his head.

'How did you learn to do that?' Emma said, unable to hide her admiration.

'Many, many years of practice.'

'Could you teach me?'

'Emma,' Abby said warningly. 'I don't think it's fair to ask.'

Mac caught Abby's eyes over the top of Emma's head.

'Why not? I'd have to teach you how to windsurf first. And I could teach Abby, too.' He raised a challenging eyebrow.

Emma's face lit up. 'Would you? That would be amazing! My dad was a windsurfer. Mum, would that be okay? Please say yes.'

Abby suppressed a groan. Emma's dad was a windsurfer right enough. This one standing in front of them. And here he was, offering to give lessons to the child he had no idea was his daughter. Under any other circumstances, Abby would have smiled. In many ways, this was exactly what she had hoped for. Daughter and father getting to know each other, but it was all happening too fast. Abby hated to refuse Emma anything, but she *had* to tell her and Mac the truth before they met again.

'We'll see. But the weather's going to start getting colder soon and then it will be winter. Perhaps it would be better to leave it until next year?' she hedged.

'But that's ages away,' Emma protested. 'I can wear a wetsuit. That'll keep me warm, won't it, Dr MacNeil?'

'Let's just see how we get on. You might decide you hate it after a go or two and that's okay. Not everyone sticks it out.'

'I will. Mum always says I stick to everything once I make up my mind, isn't that right?'

Abby ruffled her hair. 'It's true.'

'Okay, then. How about next Saturday? If the weather holds. I can pick you and your mum up.'

Emma squealed with delight before remembering she was trying to be cool these days. She clamped her hand over her mouth. 'Can I, Mum? Please say yes.'

Abby hated to refuse Emma anything and right now she couldn't think of a single reason to say no. She could always cancel the lesson later. If she had to. She shivered as the sun dropped below the horizon. 'Okay, but we'd better let Dr MacNeil get on. And I should be getting supper ready.'

'Why don't I take you girls out for something? My treat,' Mac suggested.

Behind Emma, Abby shook her head at him. The last thing she wanted right now was to have these two spending time together. At least, not until she had told them the truth.

Emma's face dropped. 'I said I would go round to Sally's house to watch a film. Her mother said she'd order pizza in for us.'

'In that case...' Mac grinned at Abby '...there's no reason why we can't go, is there?'

Abby wanted to refuse, but now that Emma and Mac had met she knew she had to speak to Mac. Putting it off would just make it harder.

'I'll have to drop Emma off at her friend's and get changed first,' she said.

'No problem. I need to go home, too. What about if I pick you up in an hour's time? We could go to the restaurant I mentioned the day we went for a walk.' Without waiting for a reply, he picked up his sailing gear and walked away, whistling.

CHAPTER FIVE

ABBY was breathing so fast that too much oxygen was making her knees weak. She would have to find the words to tell Mac that Emma was his daughter. And after that she would have to tell Emma. There was no way she could let this windsurfing lesson go ahead without both of them knowing who the other truly was.

Emma chatted about Mac and kite boarding all the way back to their little cottage. 'I can't wait to learn how he does that. How long do you think it will take me to learn? I can't believe you're working with someone as cool as him. Just wait until I tell my friends.'

Abby ached for her child. Even before knowing Mac was her father, Emma was clearly starstruck. And Abby couldn't blame her. But the very things that made him an exciting figure were the very things that could make him totally unsuitable as a father. For the umpteenth time, Abby wondered if she were about to make a dreadful mistake. Now Emma had met Mac, she'd be even more devastated if Mac wanted nothing to do with her. Whichever way Abby looked at the problem, there was no obvious right answer.

After dropping Emma off at her friend's, Abby jumped into the shower. Then she attacked her wardrobe, pulling out one outfit after another before discarding them on the floor. She told herself she wanted to look good because she needed the confidence to face Mac with her news.

Eventually she settled on a pair of dark trousers and a deep red silk blouse. A slick of dark eye shadow and the merest hint of lipstick completed her make-up. She brushed her hair until it shone and left it loose around her face, studying herself critically in the mirror. Her eyes were bright, and two spots of bright colour on her cheeks stood out against her pale skin. Suddenly she had to laugh. When Mac saw her, no doubt he would think it was the thought of going out with him that was making her look like an over-excited schoolgirl. She had to relax. Cool, calm and collected was what the occasion demanded and she knew only too well how to do cool, calm and collected. She must never let herself forget, not even for a second, that Mac was Emma's father. That fact alone made him totally out of bounds.

Hearing a knock on the door, she ran downstairs, grabbing her raincoat from the peg beside her door.

Mac smiled broadly at her when she opened the door. He had changed into dark jeans and a white shirt, which accentuated his tanned skin and the dazzling blue of his eyes. A shot of electricity ran up her spine. Despite the warning signals her brain was firing at her, her body clearly wasn't listening.

Tonight he was driving a low-slung sports car instead of the Jeep. Abby looked at him questioningly.

'The Jeep's my day car,' he said carelessly. 'This one I save for night-time. What?' He laughed, catching her look. 'I like cars. You know—boys' toys.'

He drove the same way he did everything else—fast, but with total concentration. Thankfully he slowed down on the narrow coastal roads where visibility was limited.

Nevertheless, Abby found herself gripping her seat and pumping an imaginary brake pedal as if she could slow him down.

He caught her doing it, and grinned wickedly, but he slowed the car down even further.

'Isn't it beautiful?' Abby pointed to the horizon where the sinking sun was turning the sea red. Despite the way her heart was hammering, the sight had a calming effect on her. Abby relaxed into her seat. Why *did* he have to be so attractive? She had thought he was the sexiest man she'd ever seen the first time she'd ever set eyes on him, and she still thought that. Boy, she should have got out more.

'I find everything about it beautiful,' Mac said slowly, turning his head to look at her. 'Quite stunning.'

She couldn't think of a reply, let alone force the words past a throat suddenly as dry as dust. Thankfully moments later they drew up outside a quaint-looking building. It was single storey with thick stone walls. It had been built close to the sea and as Abby stepped out of the car she gasped with pleasure. Stretching before her, as far as the eye could see, was the ocean. It was bluer than Mac's eyes and crests of white tipped the waves, which boomed like thunder as they crashed onto the shore.

Mac came to stand beside her. 'You like?' he asked, his ready smile back in place. 'See that little cove down there?' He pointed to a sandy area to Abby's left. 'That's one of my favourite places to go kite boarding.'

'You mean you surf out there? Where all those rocks are? Isn't it dangerous? Not to say foolhardy?'

Mac's grin got wider. 'Safe is boring.'

Abby craned her neck to see down to the bay. As far as she could tell, there was no path down.

'How do you get down there? I don't see a path.'

'There isn't one—that's part of the attraction. It means I always get the place to myself.'

'So how do you get to it? By boat?'

'Sometimes. Sometimes I climb down. It's more fun. It's not really that difficult—as long as you know what you're doing. One day I'll show you.'

Abby shivered at the promise behind the words. He was making it clear he found her attractive and that he expected to see more of her. Soon he would learn that it was probably going to happen, but not for the reasons he thought.

His daredevil attitude worried her. What if Emma found her father only to lose him in some reckless escapade? She was beginning to appreciate where her daughter had got her own love of risky sports from. She'd always assumed it was from Sara, but now she knew it was from both her parents. It didn't bode well for the future. She shivered again.

'You're cold. I'm sorry. Let's get inside.' He sniffed the air. Wood smoke mingled with the scent of the sea. 'Smells as if they have a fire going inside. We're early enough to grab a table that's near the fire and also has a view of the sea.'

Abby was glad he'd put her shiver down to the cold. She was already beginning to dread telling him about Emma. What if he refused to accept she was his daughter? If he did, at least this way Emma would never need know. At least, not until she was eighteen and perhaps by then she'd be able to deal with her father's rejection. But she was getting way ahead of herself. Unlikely though it seemed, perhaps he'd be pleased to find he had a child. He had been good with Tim and Luke. There was only one way to know for sure and no point in putting it off any longer.

Nevertheless, she waited until they had ordered. Mac was looking at her with the same air of puzzlement that he had shown when they'd been first introduced.

'I can't get it out of my head that we've met before. We haven't, have we? You know...' He had the grace to look embarrassed. 'No, of course we haven't. As I said, I would have remembered you.'

Abby took a deep breath. 'I lied that first day at work. We have met before. Almost twelve years ago. On Mykonos.'

Mac's frown deepened and he looked at her intently. 'Mykonos? I was there as a windsurfing instructor, but I don't... Wait a minute. I do remember you. Your hair was shorter and you wore glasses. But of course. You were there with your sister, Sara.' He leaned back in his chair and whistled. 'You've changed.'

To her fury, Abby blushed under his frank admiration. Of course he hadn't remembered her. Nobody had ever given her a second glance. Not when Sara had been around. Sara had been confident, keen to meet new people and to try out new experiences. She had thrown herself into life almost as if she'd known she wasn't long for the world. Abby had always taken on the big sister role, even though she'd only been the elder by a couple of minutes, and had never minded always being in Sara's shadow. All she'd ever wanted had been for Sara to be happy.

Abby opened her handbag and pulled out the photograph she'd put in it. She handed it to Mac. 'That's my twin, Sara. Non-identical, obviously. You have your arm around her shoulder. The one at the end is me.'

'I remember now. Hell, I haven't thought about that

summer in years. Imagine you carrying that photo around all this time' He looked at her, his dark brows drawing together. 'Why?' He half smiled. 'Don't tell me you had a crush on me and I didn't know. If so, I'm sorry. One thing's for sure, no one could fail to notice you now.'

Once again he sent her a look that gave her goose-bumps and infuriated her at the same time. Did the women he knew really fall for that kind of patter?

'How is Sara?' he continued, grinning. 'If I remember correctly, your sister knew how to have fun! Has she settled down? Sorry. That was a stupid question. Of course she has. She must be what, thirty—thirty-one?'

'Sara's dead,' Abby said bluntly.

There was no mistaking the shock on Mac's face. 'Dead! I am so sorry. When? What happened?'

'She died just over eleven years ago. About nine months after the holiday where you met.' It still sent a stab of pain through Abby whenever she had to say the words. Would she ever get used to it?

'I can't believe it! She was so full of life.' He pushed his half-eaten food away. 'I liked her very much. She was a lovely person.' Clearly he hadn't fully grasped the implication in her words.

'So fond of her you never tried getting in touch after she left?' Abby couldn't keep the bitterness from her voice. Mac had taken advantage of her sister. He had used her. Although they had both been young, he must have known that there had been a chance Sara could fall pregnant. Or had he simply not given a damn?

'Hey, I did try to get in touch, once or twice,' Mac said. 'But the phone number she left with me was never answered.' He leaned across the table, his eyes unfathomable. 'We were both young. We both accepted it was a holiday romance. Nothing more.' He placed his hand on top of Abby's. She snatched it away. Whether it was because she was still angry with him or whether it was because his touch sent little sparks of electricity shooting up her arm, she didn't want to think about.

'How did she die?' he asked softly. 'Was it an accident?'

This was the hard part. This was where she had to tell him about Emma. But suddenly she couldn't. Not yet.

'Could we talk about something else?' she asked softly. 'Even though it's been years, it still hurts too much.'

Mac was immediately contrite. 'Sure.' He leaned back in his chair and studied her intently. 'Tell me about you. How come you ended up here? Penhally is quite a change to London.'

How could she explain the change without mentioning Emma?

'I'd rather talk about you,' she said evasively. 'When we met back on Mykonos you were a windsurfing instructor. It was a bit of a shock to find you are a rescue medic.'

Mac grinned. 'Yeah, well. Back then I'd just graduated and I wanted one summer off before I started my first house job. I was fortunate. I managed to get an instructing job every summer while I was a medical student. It helped pay the bills.' For a moment his eyes darkened and he lost his ready smile. Then just as quickly the grin was back in place. 'If I couldn't be a doctor, I probably would have been a professional windsurfer. Luckily I got into medical school. Better pay and much more satisfying.'

He paused as a couple took a table close by. 'Tiree has an international reputation for some of the best surf in the world. I couldn't grow up there and not do a watersport of some description.'

'Don't tell me that's what brought you to Penhally Bay.' She didn't even attempt to hide her incredulity. What kind of doctor took a job because of the surfing conditions?

He looked amused. 'Partly. Glasgow is a great city, but I couldn't live in a place I can't kite board regularly. But I also came here because there was an opening for a medic in the air ambulance service. The job here is exactly what I always wanted.'

'You love it, don't you? The excitement and the danger. I saw the rescue you did with the family on the boat on television. You risked your life to save those people. Just as you did with Luke.'

Mac grinned again. 'It's part of the job. But you're right. I feel more alive when I battle the elements—beat the odds. But what about you? Do you think you'll cope? It must be different from what you've been used to.'

How deftly he had turned the conversation away from himself again.

'Some of it does frighten me. Especially the thought of being lowered by a winch in blustery conditions. I think it has something to do with being a mum. You know that you have a child waiting for you at home. Someone who needs you to be around for a long time, and it makes you think twice about taking risks.'

'I wouldn't know about that.' Although he smiled, a shadow crossed his eyes. 'One of the benefits about being single is that I don't have anyone who needs me. Luckily.' Abby suspected she was being warned. *Don't expect too much. I'm not in it for the long term.*

So far nothing Mac had said was what she wanted to hear.

Sensing that Mac was about to ask about Emma, Abby added quickly, 'What about your parents? Brothers? Sisters?' It wasn't just that she wanted to keep the conversation away from Emma for the time being at least, she was intensely curious. She told herself it was purely because Mac's family would be Emma's family, too.

It was as if the shutters had come down. Mac's blue eyes grew cold and distant.

'I'm an only child. I have no idea who or where my father is,' he said shortly. 'My mother still lives in Tiree. I see her when I can.'

Abby felt a tug of sympathy—and recognition. Whenever she was asked about her parents, she gave pretty much the same reply. Her father had disappeared after she and Sara had been born. He had never come back to see his daughters and the only contact they'd ever had with him had been the odd birthday card. He had died years ago, and their mother had only thought to tell Sara and Abby long after the funeral had taken place.

'But let's not talk about the past.' Mac leaned forward. 'It's the here and now that matters. I want to know more about you.'

'And the future?' Abby persisted. 'Doesn't that matter?'

Mac grinned and narrowed his eyes speculatively. 'The only thing about the future that interests me right now is when you're going to come out with me again.'

Abby returned his look coolly. Her brown eyes were reproving, almost accusing. Mac could have kicked himself. He should have known the usual direct approach wouldn't work with this woman. Instinctively he knew that Abby was someone who would expect to be courted slowly and seriously. But he didn't feel like taking things slowly with Abby. If he could have taken her home with him tonight and made love to her, he would have without a moment's hesitation.

And he didn't do serious. Abby was a woman with a child. A mother, and a protective one at that. Everything he had learned about her so far told him that she wasn't the kind of woman to have casual affairs. Why, then, was he ignoring the alarms bells that were jangling in his head?

The faint scent of her perfume drifted across at him and before he could stop himself he leaned across the table and took a lock of her thick caramel hair between his fingers. It was heavy and silky. He swallowed a groan as an image of Abby naked beside him, her hair touching his skin as she leaned over to kiss him, flashed into his head. He knew without a shadow of doubt he would never be satisfied until he had this woman in his bed.

A range of emotions he couldn't quite place crossed Abby's face. He would bet his life, though, that she felt the attraction, too.

'But the future does matter, Mac. So does the past.' She fiddled with her napkin. 'Emma...' she started. 'Sara...' She took a deep breath. Some of the colour had left her face.

'Sara died following childbirth. She developed an infection a few days after she delivered Emma. The doctors did everything they could but it was no use.' Her enormous brown eyes swam with unshed tears.

'After Emma was delivered?' Mac echoed. 'I thought Emma was your child.'

'She is. But I'm not her birth mother. Sara was. After she died, Emma came to live with me.'

Mac was puzzled. Why was she telling him this? It did explain, however, why there was no father in the picture. Despite everything he'd just told himself, he couldn't help feeling glad.

'Sara delivered Emma nine months after she returned from Mykonos.' Abby caught her bottom lip between her teeth.

Did she have any idea how cute she looked when she did that?

'Mac, Emma is your daughter.'

Emma? His daughter? At least he thought that was what Abby said. He must have misheard.

'Did I hear you correctly?' he said. He hoped to hell he hadn't.

'Yes. I didn't know at first. Sara wouldn't tell me who the father was, although, given the timing, I had my suspicions.'

'So she might not be mine?' He heard the relief in his voice.

'She didn't tell me it was you until she knew for certain she was going to die. Then she confirmed what I had suspected all along. You were the father.'

Mac felt as if he was in a nightmare. He couldn't have a daughter. It was impossible. God knew, he didn't want one. He would make a terrible father anyway. His mind was racing. Admittedly, Sara and he had spent almost the whole fortnight together and, yes, they'd had sex. Neither of them had ever pretended that what they'd shared had been anything more than a holiday romance. And he remembered he had asked about contraception. He hadn't been such an idiot as to have unprotected sex. Although Sara had insisted she was on the Pill, they had used condoms, too. In his twenty-one years he had hardly been a saint and he hadn't taken chances with anyone's sexual health. So how could she have fallen pregnant? But then it came back to him. There had been one evening after a beach party when they'd both had too much to drink and they hadn't used condoms. It had never crossed his mind that Sara could have become pregnant. He forced himself to focus on what Abby was saying.

'When Emma was three months old, I went back to Mykonos to try and find you, but it was no use. You were gone. All I knew was that you were called Mac. I asked around, but nobody could tell me anything that would help me trace you.'

'That summer was my last of teaching windsurfing. After that I was too busy doing my house jobs. I didn't need the money or, more to the point, have the time.' He still felt dazed. 'You can't be sure she's mine, whatever Sara told you.'

'Think about it, Mac. Sara had no reason to lie. If she had wanted to, she could have told you she was pregnant, but she didn't. It was only when she knew she was going to die that she told me. And that was only because she knew that one day Emma would want to know something about her father. Possibly find him.' She paused. 'But if you still have your doubts I'm sure we can arrange a DNA test.' Although that wasn't what she wanted. Emma would be hurt to find out that the father she so desperately wanted had needed proof that she was his daughter.

'I think that might be a good idea.' Mac stumbled to his feet. He had to get out of there. He needed time to think. He saw his life changing in front of his eyes. A father!

'Mac, I know this has been a shock to you. It was to me when I realised I would be working with you. At least, in my case, I've known about you for years.'

'Does Emma know? That I'm her father, I mean?'

'She knows that her father is out there somewhere. She doesn't know it's you. Not yet. I thought it was only fair to talk to you first.'

'Will you tell her?'

'Yes. She desperately wants to find her father.' Abby reached out and touched him on the hand. 'Mac, please sit down. I can't think with you standing over me like that.'

Reluctantly Mac did as she asked. He owed it to Abby to hear her out, however much he didn't want to believe what she was telling him.

'The reason I took the job here was because Emma was being bullied at her school in London. You know how cruel kids can be. When they found out that Em didn't know who her father was they started teasing her. They wouldn't even come to her eleventh birthday party. Things just got worse from there.'

Ouch. Mac remembered only too well how that felt. Growing up in a small community, as he had done, it had been exactly the same for him, but at least he'd had his windsurfing. Out on the waves he'd been able to forget everything. Besides, his skill on the board had made him a bit of a hero in the other children's eyes. But their teasing had still hurt. He felt a rush of sympathy towards Emma. And anger. How dared those children pick on a little girl about something that was out of her control? If he had them in front of them right now, he'd be tempted to bang their heads together.

'If it turns out I am Emma's father, I won't deny her,'

he said. 'I'll do what's right. Provide financial support, whatever you need.'

Abby's eyes flashed with anger. 'Financial support isn't what is needed, Mac. Emma and I manage fine. What Emma needs is far more complicated than that. As soon as she knows about you she is going to want a relationship. Can you give her that?'

Right now, Mac had no idea.

Mac got to his feet again. 'I'm sorry, Abby, I just don't know if I can do what you're asking. I never wanted to be a father. I don't have the first clue about being one. There's a good chance I'll be rubbish at it. Emma is probably better off without me.' He jammed his hands into his pockets. 'I need time to think about this. Decide what to do.'

'Don't think too long, Mac. I have to tell Emma that I've found you.' She got to her feet, too. 'You said you'd take her windsurfing next Saturday. Whether you show up or not is up to you.'

He could see the determination in her calm nut-brown eyes.

'But let me warn you. If you do decide to get involved with her, it's not something you can back out of later. You're in it for keeps. Make no mistake, Mac, if you hurt my child, you'll have me to reckon with.'

CHAPTER SIX

MAC let himself into his flat and flung his car keys on the table. He had dropped Abby back home and they had sat in silence the whole of the journey. He was still reeling from what Abby had told him. There he'd been thinking he had been doing nothing more than taking a beautiful woman out to dinner. Now it seemed as if he was father to that woman's daughter!

He thought back to when he had seen Emma on the beach. She was tall—like him. And she had blue eyes—like him. But was that enough to go on?

He crossed over to his full-length windows and stared out to sea. How could his life have changed so dramatically in just a matter of hours? The last thing he wanted, or needed, was an eleven-year-old daughter. Why hadn't Sara told him she was pregnant? He felt a grudging respect for the woman who had given birth to his child. She had known how much his medical career had meant to him. She had also probably known, he admitted ruefully, that back then he had not been up to being a father. But was he up to it now?

The wind had risen, whipping the sea against the rocks. He wished he was out there, challenging himself against the elements. It was so much easier than dealing with the bomb Abby had thrown at him.

He poured himself a whisky and swirled the amber liquid around the glass. Memories of his own childhood came rushing back. The endless stream of men his mother had brought home, insisting that he call them Dad. He had refused. And just as well; none of them, except Dougie, had lasted more than a couple of months. Mac had got on with him. It had been Dougie who had given him his first second-hand board and Mac would have considered calling him Dad, but eventually Dougie had left, too, driven away by his mother's excessive demands. She had blamed Mac. Told him that he had ruined her chances of finding happiness. No wonder he had learned to windsurf. The time on the waves had been his only relief from his bitter, resentful mother. That, and school. As soon as he'd been able to, he had left home, supporting himself through medical school by taking out loans and teaching windsurfing. It had been hard. There had been too many times when he'd had to choose between buying a textbook and eating. But he'd survived, learning to depend on only himself. No wonder he'd never let anyone get close to him and so far it had worked out exactly the way he wanted. He was living the perfect life. A job he loved, this flat, mountain biking, free climbing and kite boarding whenever he could, and dating the kind of women who seemed happy to fit in around his other pleasures.

Until now.

He took a swig of his whisky, letting the liquid roll around his tongue. His life was going to be turned upside down. But what if Sara had been wrong? What if Emma wasn't his child? He had to know for certain one way or another. If she was his, he wouldn't abandon her. He couldn't do the same thing to a child, his child, as his father had done to him. At least Emma had Abby. An image of hazel eyes and a warm smile floated in front of his eyes. She was the opposite of the women he normally went after. She was serious, warm, caring and fiercely protective. He knew instinctively she would be like a tigress when it came to protecting her daughter. Abby, he was sure, would never have told him he was Emma's father if she hadn't been certain of it herself. She had taken a risk telling him and she knew it. Sighing, he placed his empty glass on the table and reached for the phone. He had to see Abby and arrange the DNA test after she had a chance to tell Emma. The sooner he knew for sure that Emma was his, the better for all concerned. But deep down he was getting used to the idea. Already he felt something strange, a sense of protectiveness towards the young girl who Abby claimed was his child.

Abby finished tidying the kitchen while listening to Emma's excited chatter. It was so good to see the little girl back to her usual self.

'Emma, I need to talk to you about something,' Abby said when Emma drew breath. 'Why don't I make us a cup of cocoa and we can take it in to the sitting room and chat there?'

When they were settled, Abby turned to Emma.

'You know how we spoke about your dad? Remember I told you I tried to find him when you were very little?'

Emma nodded and waited for Abby to continue.

'Well, I've found him.'

'Where? Who is he? How did you find him? Did he come looking for me?' The hope in Emma's eyes made Abby's heart stumble.

'He couldn't look for you, sweetie, because he didn't

know about you. I kind of found him by accident.' Abby took a deep breath. There was no going back now.

'You know Dr MacNeil? The man we met on the beach? He's your father.'

Emma looked stunned. 'Dr MacNeil? I thought you said my dad was a windsurfer.'

'Well, he is. We saw that down on the beach, but he's also a doctor. He taught windsurfing as a way to put himself through medical school.'

A slow smile crept across Emma's face. 'That's so cool. Does he know? Did you tell him? What did he say?'

Abby smiled at Emma's excitement. 'Yes, he knows. I told him.' Abby leaned across and took Emma's hand in hers. 'It was a bit of a surprise to him. He had no idea that your mother had even been pregnant. I guess it'll take him a little time to get used to the idea he has a daughter.'

Emma's brow puckered. 'You mean he doesn't want me.'

Abby took the mug from Emma and placed it on the coffee table, before pulling her daughter into her arms. 'Of course he'll want you. He just needs time to get to know you better. You and I have always known that you had a dad out there somewhere, but this has all come as a big surprise to him.'

'Is he still going to take me windsurfing?'

'I'm not sure. Em, don't get your hopes up too much. Remember when we've spoken about this before, we always said that even if we found your father, he might not want to be as involved as you might hope.'

'I don't care,' Emma said fiercely. 'I know I've always got you.' She sat up, her brows furrowing. 'This won't make any difference to us, will it? I mean, you'll always be my mum, won't you? He can't take me away from you, even if he wants to, right?'

Abby had wondered the same thing herself. When Sara had died, Abby had thought about adopting Emma officially, but it hadn't seem to be necessary. The social services had been more than happy to leave Emma in her care. Surely, and Abby thought this was unlikely, even if Mac did want to have Emma with him full time, no one would give him custody?

'I don't think that's going to happen. You're my daughter and no one is ever going to take you away from me. Look, let's take this one day at a time. You and Mac can get to know each other and we'll take it from there.'

Emma nodded. 'At least the kids won't be able to tease me about not having a father any more.' She hugged Abby. 'I can't wait to meet him properly. What's he like? Tell me everything you know.'

Emma was too excited to go to bed and she and Abby talked into the night. Abby brought out all her old photos of Sara and repeated the stories of their childhood that Emma could never get enough of. Finally she was able to persuade an exhausted but happy Emma to go to bed. Looking down at her sleeping child, Abby made a vow: Dr William MacNeil would not be allowed to cause her daughter so much as a moment's pain.

Early the next morning, there was a knock on the door. Abby opened it to find Mac standing there, an uncertain smile on his face.

'Can I come in?'

Abby was glad Emma was still in bed, catching up on sleep after their late night.

She stood back to let him in.

He brushed past her and started pacing her small

sitting room. He only managed a couple of strides in each direction before he had to turn round.

'Have you told her?' He hadn't even said hello.

'Yes. Last night.'

'How did she take the news?' He seemed nervous, uncharacteristically unsure of himself.

'She was thrilled. I warned her that I didn't know what you were going to do about it.'

'I'm not going to ask for a DNA test,' Mac said abruptly.

'Oh? Why not?' Had he made up his mind that regardless of whether it could be proven Emma was his child, he still didn't want to know? Abby's heart gave a sickening thud. It would be hard telling Emma, but perhaps it was for the best. In that case, either Mac or she and Emma would have to leave Cornwall. It would be too cruel for Emma to be reminded daily that she had a father who didn't want her.

'I don't want a DNA test because it's not fair to Emma. You say she's my child. The dates fit. She looks like me. If I insist on a DNA test, how will that make her feel? I know that if I were in her shoes, I would think that my father was trying to prove I wasn't his. No child deserves to be put through that.'

'So what are you saying, Mac? I'm afraid you're going to have to spell it out.'

'Look, I don't know what sort of father I'll make, but I'm going to give it my best shot. You and Emma will just have to be patient with me. Can you do that, Abby? Can you accept I can only do the best I can? That it might not be good enough?'

Abby was relieved he wasn't insisting on a DNA test. But as far as what kind of father he would be? Well, that was up to him. It wasn't as if she could go and pick him up a set of instructions from some kind of parent supermarket.

'Just promise me you'll do the best you can,' she said softly.

He sighed. 'You're going to have to help me here, Abby. As I said, I have no idea how to go about being a father. I mean, what do I do?'

He looked so different from his usual confident self that Abby's heart melted a little.

'I think taking her windsurfing is a good start,' she said. 'That way you and Emma can get to know each other without it seeming forced and unnatural.'

'I can do that. What else?'

'Let's just take it day by day, Mac. Learning to be a father takes time.'

'Tell Emma I'll see her on Saturday.' And with that he turned on his heel and was out the door as if the devil himself were after him.

CHAPTER SEVEN

MAC took a gulp of his beer as he waited for Josh to emerge from the changing room. It had been a good match, even if it had been closer than Mac would have liked. Shortly after Mac had started working on the air ambulance crew, Josh had invited him to join the five-a-side football team that many of the staff at the hospital played for. In the end, their team had just pulled the match out of the bag. Mac was pleased. He hated to lose.

'I got one in for you,' he told Josh when he appeared, gesturing towards the pint he had placed on the table.

After the match, the team would have a quick pint and usually talk about work. For various reasons tonight it was just him and Josh who'd stayed for a drink. Everyone else had had reasons to rush away, but although Josh was married he never seemed in a hurry to leave after the game.

Mac knew little about Josh's personal life. He had met his wife, Rebecca, once or twice when she had dropped into A & E to see her husband. Mac had got the impression that Rebecca was a little lonely. The life as a wife of a consultant could be like that, especially if, like Rebecca, she didn't work. Another reason to stay footloose and fancy-free, Mac decided—except he wasn't, not any more.

'How's Rebecca?' Mac asked. 'Does she like living here?'

Josh studied his pint glass as he twirled it around in his hand. 'I think Rebecca is more of a city girl. She misses being able to pop into the shops any time she pleases.'

'Yet she agreed to move here?' Mac said.

'It was too good an opportunity for me to miss. Hopefully in time Rebecca will make friends. Although it's difficult when she doesn't work. Not having children doesn't help either. If we had kids, she'd probably meet some mothers down at the school gates.'

'If you're planning on having some, I wouldn't leave it too long. How old is Rebecca? Thirty-three? Thirty-four?'

Josh frowned. 'Thirty-four. But we always agreed they weren't part of the plan.'

The expression on Josh's face darkened for a moment. What's going on here? Mac thought. But whatever it was, it was none of his business. Josh and Rebecca's private life had nothing to do with him.

'Anyway, what about you? I guess you're not the father type either. Or haven't you met the right woman yet?'

Mac shifted in his seat. Served him right. He had started this conversation. Besides, people were bound to find out sooner or later.

'Er… Actually, it turns out I am a father,' he said. The words sounded strange, still unbelievable.

Josh's eyebrows shot up. 'You kept that quiet. A bit of a dark horse, aren't you?'

'I only just found out myself.' If it were possible,

Josh looked even more astonished. But he said nothing, simply waited for Mac to continue.

'It's complicated,' Mac said. 'You know our new paramedic, Abby Stevens?'

'She's the mother of your child?' Josh's eyebrows couldn't go any higher.

'No. She's the aunt of my child. Emma, my daughter, is the result of a relationship I had with Abby's twin—years ago.'

'I think you're going to have to be more explicit,' Josh said, leaning back in his chair. 'Go on, I'm all ears.'

Mac wasn't used to talking about himself, but he had to tell someone. Perhaps thinking out loud would help. So, hesitantly, between sips of beer, he told Josh the whole story.

'And you had no idea Sara was pregnant?' A shadow crossed Josh's face, making Mac wonder, but he kept his thoughts to himself.

'None. It never crossed my mind.'

'And you believe Abby?'

'If you knew Abby better, you'd know that's a daft question. She's not the kind of woman to lie about something like this. She's totally upfront. With Abby, what you see is what you get.'

Josh raised an eyebrow again. There was a hint of a smile at the corner of his mouth. Mac wanted to tell him that he was mistaken, that there was nothing between him and Abby, but he knew his protests would only increase that amused look in Josh's eyes.

'Besides, it is entirely possible. The timing works out. And I was young at the time. Not always as responsible as I should have been.'

Josh's frown deepened. Did he disapprove? Surely Josh must have behaved in ways he now regretted when he had been a medical student. But perhaps Josh had been sensible enough always to take precautions. As medics, they knew better. Or, at least in his case, should have known better. But, damn it, he wasn't asking Josh for his approval. 'Shortly before she died, Sara told Abby I was the father and I can see no reason why Sara would lie. Besides, Emma has my eyes. I don't think there's much doubt.'

'So what are you going to do about it?'

'No idea, Josh. It's not as if I planned to be a father. I'm pretty sure I'll make a rotten one. But I can't turn away from my responsibilities. I told Abby that I'll spend time with Emma. I'm going to teach her to windsurf. At least I can do that.'

Josh looked thoughtful. He put his glass down on the table and leaned forward. 'You know, Mac, sometimes life deals us a hand we never wanted, or expected. We get one chance at grabbing what's in front of us. If we don't take it while we can, it might be a mistake we end up regretting for the rest of our lives.'

Something in his voice made Mac wonder if he was speaking from personal experience, but before he could decide whether to probe further, Josh went on. 'If I were you, I would think very carefully before you turn away from something that might turn out to be the best thing that's ever happened to you.'

'It sounds as if you know what you're talking about,' Mac said.

'Let's just say, if I had a particular time over in my life, I might have made different choices.' Josh picked up his and Mac's empty glasses. He nodded in the direction of the bar. 'Fancy a refill?' he asked.

On the way home Mac thought about what Josh had said. There was a mystery there, he was sure of it, but he respected his colleague too much to speculate on what it could be. If he wanted him to know, he'd tell him. As far as his advice about Abby and Emma went—that was different. He had promised Abby that he would get to know Emma and he had never gone back on his promise. But the thought still scared him witless. What did he know about being a father? He hadn't exactly had a good example himself. Unless it had been how not to be a father. His father had walked out on him and his mother without a backward glance. Walking out of the marriage had been one thing, but abandoning your only child had been quite another.

He swallowed his anger. It was no use thinking like that. What he did have to think about was *his* child. Whatever the future brought, however much he hadn't planned on having a child and however much disruption that might bring to the life he had carved out for himself, there was really no choice. He was Emma's father and he wouldn't—couldn't—abandon her.

CHAPTER EIGHT

THE next couple of days were busy, and Mac and Abby were seldom alone together, for which Mac was grateful.

He was still getting used to the fact that he had a daughter and almost as strange was that Abby was the mother of his child. For the first time in his life he was confused by his feelings for a woman.

He liked working with Abby. He admired the way she was with the patients: calm, assured but gentle, as if they really mattered to her.

They had the usual callouts to walkers with broken ankles that turned out to be badly twisted, and a couple of car accidents that thankfully turned out to be less serious than initially thought. When there wasn't a call-out, the team went over rescue procedures and updated each other with new medical developments. Mac was careful to treat Abby like simply another member of the team.

It wasn't easy. He'd come to recognise the habit she had of biting her lip whenever she was anxious, and more than once he had to stop himself from leaning across and brushing a lock of hair from her eyes. He could hardly keep his eyes off her. He loved the way her mouth curved and her eyes lit up when she was pleased about something and he resented the way he kept imagining what it would be like to feel her mouth on his. Okay, so she was beautiful and sexy and warm but now he knew about Emma, Abby was out of bounds. He already had one commitment he had never expected and he didn't need another.

It was just after lunch on Wednesday when they received a call to attend a woman who had been thrown off her horse and then trampled. The only information they had to go on was that the woman was unconscious and in a field with no road access. The call had been transferred to the RAF, which was sending out a Sea King so that the medics could be winched down to the casualty if necessary

Within minutes Abby and Mac were being flown towards the injured woman.

'This could be nasty,' Mac said into his radio. 'If she's unconscious, it'll be difficult for us to be sure just how badly injured she is.'

'In that case, don't we treat her as if she has a spinal injury?' Abby asked.

'The most important thing is to keep her breathing,' Mac agreed. 'And not to make things worse.'

Ten short minutes later they were hovering over the accident site. A man was standing next to the woman, waving a brightly coloured jacket to get their attention.

'As we thought, there's nowhere to put down, I'm afraid,' the pilot said. 'It's too marshy. You're going to have to be winched out.'

Mac glanced at Abby and was surprised to see a flash of fear in her eyes.

'Are you okay?'

Abby nibbled her lip. 'It's the first time other than

training that I've had to winch down. I'm just a little nervous.'

'Tell you what,' he said. 'Seeing there is someone on board that can lower us both, why don't we go down together? That way we can get down quicker.' It wouldn't really make much difference timewise, but going down in tandem would make Abby feel better. It was the first time she had revealed a less than certain side to her and it made him feel unusually protective. Whether it was because she was the mother of his child or because this woman engendered feelings he had never experienced before, he didn't want to think about. He much preferred to think it was the former.

Mac stood and attached the winch to the harness they always wore in the helicopter. Although she was determined not to show it, Abby was relieved he'd be going down with her. She was intensely aware of the touch of his hands on her legs and hips as he tested the buckles.

The last few days he had been polite but distant towards her. When she'd asked him whether he still intended to take Emma windsurfing, he'd looked surprised. 'I don't go back on promises, Abby,' he'd said. 'Especially not to a child.'

They were lowered over the side, pressed together, one of Mac's arms holding her close. This was almost worse than going down alone. Her fear disappeared under her awareness of his hard, muscular body touching every inch of hers. She raised her head to look at him and he winked. She wasn't sure whether she was glad or disappointed when they touched the ground and Mac released them from the winch. All she knew was that her body felt as if it was on fire and that the blood was whooshing in her ears.

Mac raced to the fallen woman, leaving Abby to follow in his wake.

He crouched down beside her, feeling for a pulse. Then he used the small torch they all carried in the top pockets of their jumpsuits to shine a light in her eyes. Abby's heart sank when she saw that only one pupil reacted to the light.

'How long since it happened?' Mac asked the man who had stayed with her.

'I don't know, but not long before I found her. She cantered past me a few minutes earlier. I lost sight of her but then I saw her horse galloping away without a rider, so I knew something had happened. I telephoned for help immediately.' He looked at his watch. 'About twenty-five minutes ago. So I would estimate it's been approximately half an hour since she fell.'

'Has she been conscious at all? Have you moved her, Mr...?'

'Fox. No, I know you're not supposed to. I had some medical training when I was in the army. I just checked that she was breathing.'

Abby slipped a neck brace out of her bag. Although the head injury was their primary concern, they had to assume until they knew otherwise that the victim had a spinal injury, too.

Mac nodded and working together they slipped the brace round the fallen woman's neck and an oxygen mask over her face.

Then they strapped the rider's legs together to make the transfer to the helicopter. With Mr Fox helping, they slipped the two halves of the stretcher underneath her.

Mac was winched into the helicopter with the stretcher and a short time later the line was dropped again. Her heart thudding, Abby attached herself and gave the thumbs-up signal to be lifted. She could hardly ask Mac to leave their patient and come back for her. But to her relief the upward lift was okay. Having done it on the way down with Mac had helped. Abby knew that from now on she would never again worry about that part of the rescue, and she had Mac's thoughtfulness to thank for that.

Back in the helicopter, Mac had already attached their patient to the onboard monitoring system and was gently feeling her abdomen. As he did so, Abby noted some swelling just below the woman's ribs. She glanced up at Mac, who was shaking his head and looking worried.

'Damage to the spleen?' she asked.

He nodded. 'The sooner we get her to hospital the better. If she has ruptured her spleen she'll need surgery as soon as possible. I'll radio ahead and let them know so they can have the surgeons and a theatre standing by.'

The next ten minutes were tense as Abby continued to monitor the woman's vital signs and neuro observations. Her pulse was rapid, making the possibility of a ruptured spleen more likely. Mac helped Abby put up a drip. Giving the injured woman fluids would help keep her stabilised in the short term.

Abby sighed with relief when the helicopter landed gently on the landing pad at the hospital. As before, they were met by the A & E team. There was no time for introductions as they wheeled the woman straight into Resus and Abby stepped back, allowing the A & E team to take over. As they carried out their own assessment, Mac relayed what he and Abby had done so far.

'I think you're right about the ruptured spleen, Mac,' the dark-haired emergency consultant who had loaned them his car told them. 'Could I have a portable ultrasound over here, please?' While the A & E consultant prepared to scan the victim's abdomen, Mac was checking her reflexes. 'Right pupil still blown,' he said. 'I suspect a subdural haematoma, Josh. We should get the neurosurgeons down here to have a look.'

'I'm here.'

Abby whirled around to see a Latin-looking man enter the room. He crossed over to the trolley and Mac stepped aside to allow him to examine the rider. By this time the resus room was crowded. Apart from Dr Corezzi, the neurosurgeon, and Josh, there were several other people in the room, all occupied with the patient.

Mac passed an endotracheal tube down the woman's throat.

'Okay, let's get her to Theatre. The spleen *is* ruptured so she's going to need that fixed, too,' Josh said quietly. Despite his calm voice, Abby knew they were worried. A few moments later the woman was being wheeled out of the room to Theatre.

The emergency over, Josh and Mac peeled off their gloves.

'That was close,' Josh said. 'It was a good thing you were there, Mac. It makes a difference knowing in advance what we might be dealing with. This is exactly the type of case where having a doctor attached to the ambulance service makes a difference.'

'You're right. But whether a few successful cases will persuade the powers that be that having a full-time doctor attached to the service makes financial sense is a different story. She still might not make it,' Mac replied. 'But at least she has a chance.'

Mac glanced over at Abby, seeming surprised to see her still standing there. 'I couldn't have done it without

Abby. Abby, this is Dr Josh O'Hara, one of the A & E consultants here. Josh, this is Abby, our new paramedic, who has joined us from the London service.'

Josh grinned. 'We're lucky to have you.'

Abby took in his dark hair and ready smile. He was very good-looking, but for some reason he did nothing to her pulse. Unlike Mac. Unfortunately.

'Have you had a chance to look around St Piran's, Abby?' Josh asked.

Abby smiled. 'Not yet. There hasn't really been time. But I'd really like to go to the special care nursery. I have a patient there I'd like to see.'

'I have to pop into ITU,' Mac said. 'Josh, if you're not busy, perhaps you could take Abby up to Special Care? I'll meet you there in five.'

'Sure. No probs. I'll just let the nursing staff know where I am. I can introduce you to whoever is on duty at the same time, Abby.'

There were too many faces for Abby to take in, but everyone welcomed her warmly. She couldn't help but notice that Josh caused quite a stir in the department. There were several wistful looks in his direction of which he seemed oblivious. After they left the department, Josh took Abby upstairs to the SCBU. A nurse met them as they entered.

Josh introduced Abby. 'Abby was the paramedic who helped Mrs Hargreaves when she went into labour. She wanted to say hello and see how the baby's getting on.'

'Mum is with the baby now and they are both doing fine. It would have been a different story if you and Dr MacNeil hadn't got them here so quickly.' She peered over Abby's shoulder, as if expecting to find Mac standing behind her. She looked disappointed to find he wasn't. The nurse pointed to a cot near the middle of the room. 'They're over there if you want to go over.'

'Is Dr Phillips on duty?' Josh asked.

'Megan? Yes. Isn't she always? She's in the staffroom, catching up on paperwork.'

Josh looked at Abby. 'That's where I'll be if you need me. Mac should be along shortly.'

Abby found Jenny sitting by the cot, gazing down at her baby. As soon as she noticed Abby, her face broke into an enormous smile.

'How's he doing?' Abby whispered, peering into the cot. A tiny infant lay in it, his nappy almost taking up half of his small body. There were a few lines snaking from his tiny hands and feet, but he was breathing on his own. That was a good sign.

'He's doing okay. They think I'll be able to take him home in a week or two. And it's all thanks to you and Dr MacNeil. The staff say that if I'd been any later getting to hospital I might have lost him—or died, too. I don't know how to thank you enough.' Her voice cracked slightly. She had been through a very stressful experience and was bound to still be worried.

'You don't have to thank us. It's our job. I'm just thrilled that it all worked out okay.' Abby held out her arms and Jenny passed her sleeping child to her. Abby breathed in the particular blissful scent of baby.

Jenny was looking at something over Abby's shoulder. Abby turned round to find Mac standing there, looking at them. Jenny smiled and waved him over.

Mac approached them slowly, looking as if he'd rather be anywhere else than there.

'Dr MacNeil, I'm so glad I caught you. I wanted to thank you personally for saving my baby. And for taking care of Tim. I know he had his brave face on, but he was truly terrified until you came along.'

Mac shuffled his feet, looking uncomfortable. 'As I'm sure Abby told you, it was nothing. All in a day's work. How is Tim anyway?'

'He's at school today. His dad will bring him up later. He's totally besotted with his little brother. He kind of feels that he almost helped deliver him. He was a bit embarrassed when he first heard I was pregnant—you know how young boys can be about that sort of stuff— but now he couldn't be prouder.'

Just then Josh approached them, accompanied by a woman with russet hair and fine, delicate features.

'Abby, this is Dr Megan Phillips—one of the paediatric registrars,' Josh introduced her.

'Hi, Abby. I've heard all about you from Mrs Hargreaves here. I understand that it's thanks to you our latest miracle baby is doing well,' Megan said.

'Would you like to hold him, Dr Phillips?' Jenny asked. 'And seeing as you're all here, I might take the opportunity to pop to the bathroom.'

But Abby was surprised when Megan blanched. Instead, Josh stepped forward and took the tiny infant in his arms, cradling him with practised ease.

'Hey, Josh,' Mac teased. 'Looks like you're a natural after all. Are you practising for when you and Rebecca have kids? The nurses in A & E tell me that's all she talks about when she visits the department. You'd better make the most of the next few months. One of these days you'll be up to your ears in nappies.'

'Not me, I'm afraid,' Josh said lightly.

Abby saw Josh and Megan exchange a look. It was brief, the merest glance, but the paediatric registrar's face went even whiter. If she hadn't known Josh was married to Rebecca, Abby would have sworn there was something between the two doctors. But perhaps her own situation was making her hypersensitive. That was all.

As soon as Jenny returned Megan made her excuses. 'I'll be back to check on this little one in a while,' she told the happy mother. 'But if you'll excuse me, right now I have other patients to look in on.' She smiled, but Abby could see it didn't quite reach her eyes. After a brief nod at the two men, she left the ward.

'I should be getting back to A & E,' Josh said, handing the baby back to his mother. 'So if you'll excuse me, too? Abby, it was good to meet you. I'm sure we'll meet again soon.'

'We should go, too, Abby,' Mac said.

'No problem. If someone could just point me in the direction of the bathroom first? It was lovely to see you again, Jenny. And your baby. We don't always get the chance to catch up with our patients, so when we do, it's a real pleasure.'

'Thank you both, again.' She gazed down at her sleeping child, who was just beginning to stir. 'Looks like he's ready for a feed.'

'The bathroom's just outside the swing doors, Abby,' Mac said. 'I'll meet you downstairs.'

Abby found the bathroom. To her surprise Megan was leaning against the basin, her face streaked with tears. Concerned, Abby moved towards her and touched her on the arm.

'Megan? What's wrong?'

Megan managed a wan smile and leaned over the sink to splash her face with water. 'Don't mind me. I'm just having one of those days.'

'Are you sure there's nothing I can do?'

Megan reached for a paper towel to pat her face dry. 'No, really. But I'd appreciate it if you kept this to yourself. It doesn't seem too professional for the doctor to be found crying in the bathroom.'

'We all have our moments,' Abby said, 'when stuff gets on top of us.' She paused. 'Look, I'm new here and I haven't really met many people yet, and I'm always up for a bit of adult female company. Why don't you come over for supper one night?'

Megan smiled. She really is beautiful, Abby thought. But her eyes are so sad. Something was bothering her and it was more than just an off day, Abby would have staked her life on it.

'I would like that,' Megan said.

Abby wrote down her address and mobile number and passed it to Megan.

'Phone me?'

'Sure,' Megan said, pocketing the number. But somehow Abby didn't think she would.

CHAPTER NINE

ABBY woke early on Saturday morning to find that Emma was up before her. That in itself was unusual. She normally had to call Em at least twice before she could get her out of bed. Even more unusual was the smell of toast drifting from the kitchen. Moments later Emma appeared by her bed, carrying a tray with tea and buttered toast.

'Hey, what's this?' Abby said, sitting up and taking the tray.

'I woke up really early. I couldn't stay in bed so I thought I'd make you breakfast for a change.'

Emma's eyes were bright with excitement and it worried Abby. Perhaps she shouldn't have told her about Mac? Maybe she should have waited to see how the relationship developed? What if after today Mac backed away from having anything to do with his daughter? Abby knew the rejection would break Emma's heart. But what was the alternative? Lying to Emma? One way or another her daughter would have found out about Mac. Maybe not straight away, but eventually. And then how would she have felt about Abby keeping the truth from her? That would have been worse. One of the things Abby had always promised Em was that she would never lie to her.

Emma was dressed, with her long blonde hair, so like Sara's, tied back in a ponytail. She crept into bed beside Abby. 'When do you think he'll be here?' she asked.

Abby glanced at her watch and groaned. It was only six-thirty.

'Not for a little while. I think he said eight.'

'What if he doesn't come?' Emma asked anxiously.

'He'll come,' Abby promised. Or he'll have me to answer to, she thought grimly. But somehow she knew that once Mac had made a decision he would stick to it.

'Are you coming, too?' Emma asked.

'Do you want me to?'

'I think so,' Emma said.

'Then I will.' Abby tossed the bedclothes aside and jumped out of bed. 'But there is no way I'm going to try windsurfing. The sea's far too cold for me.'

Emma grinned up at her. 'Don't be such a wuss. We'll be wearing wetsuits. Come on, Mum. You have to give it a go. It'll be fun.'

'We'll see,' Abby said evasively. 'Right now, I need a shower.'

Bang on eight o'clock there was a knock on the door. Abby opened it to find Mac standing there, looking almost as nervous as Emma. He had a bunch of flowers in his hand. 'I brought these for Emma,' he said. 'To be honest, I didn't know what the form was for meeting one's daughter officially for the first time.'

Abby smiled. 'She'll be delighted. I don't think anyone's given her flowers before.' She took the bouquet from him. 'Emma!' she called out. 'Mac's here.' As she stood aside to let Mac into the small hall she added, 'I think Mac is best at this stage, don't you?'

Mac nodded, craning his neck to look behind her.

'Hi, Mac,' Emma said from behind her.

'Mac brought these flowers for you. I'll put them in water before we go, shall I?'

Emma's smile lit up her face. 'Flowers. Wicked. Thank you, Mac.'

Mac bowed slightly in acknowledgement. 'It is my pleasure. Have you got your costume and something warm to put on after your lesson? We'll be warm enough while we're moving, but when we get out of the water, you might get cold.'

Emma nodded. 'Mum's already been through all that. She's coming, too. She said she might even try it herself.'

Mac raised an eyebrow. 'Good for her.' He paused. 'Did you know I taught Sara how to windsurf?'

Emma nodded again. 'Mum told me. She said that's how you and my real mum met. Was she good at it?'

Abby's heart cracked a little. Emma was so desperate for any titbits about Sara. Abby had told her as much as she could about her, leaving out the bits about Sara's wild side, concentrating on the warm, fun-loving side of Sara. The only reason Sara had taken windsurfing lessons had been to get to know Mac. As far as Abby knew, once Sara and Mac had become an item, Sara had given up windsurfing, preferring to sit on the beach and watch.

'She wasn't bad.' Mac grinned. 'But she didn't take the lessons for very long.' Abby was grateful to Mac for his tactful answer. 'I have a feeling you're going to take to it.'

Ten minutes later they were on the almost deserted beach, and only the real die-hard surfers were out on the waves. While Emma was getting changed, Mac popped into one of the surfing shops that hired out equipment and returned with a couple of wetsuits. 'I brought one for you,' he told Abby, 'in case you do give it a shot. 'I'm just going to get a beginner's board for Emma then we'll be set.'

Abby was getting the distinct impression she wasn't going to be allowed off the hook.

By the time Emma appeared, wrapped in her towel and shivering in the cool morning air, Mac had organised a board for her. He handed her a wetsuit and helped her into it.

'Okay, this first bit we do on land. Abby can join in without getting changed. All she needs to do is slip off her shoes.'

Just as she'd suspected, Abby thought ruefully. There was no getting out of it. She undid the laces of her trainers and removed her socks. The sand squirmed pleasantly between her toes.

'Okay, Emma. Pop onto the board. I'll show you how you lift the sail and how to balance yourself. Then we'll have a go on the water.'

Emma got the hang of the basics pretty quickly. 'It will be more difficult in the sea,' Mac warned, 'but so far I'm impressed. Now, Abby, how about you having a go?'

Reluctantly, Abby stepped on the board and, following Mac's instructions, tugged on the sail to try and lift it. It was harder than she had expected. Determined to do it, she pulled with all her strength and almost toppled over when the sail whooshed up towards her. But Mac had anticipated her losing her balance and she felt strong hands circle her waist, steadying her. The feel of his hands cupping her waist sent all kinds of sensations shooting through her body and she prayed neither he nor

Emma noticed the heat that rushed to her face. The last thing she wanted or needed was to have such a physical reaction to this man and, even worse, for either of them to notice.

Mac remained behind her, close enough for every cell in her body to be acutely aware of him. His breath tickled her neck as he placed his hands over hers, showing her how to hold the board. She was getting more and more flustered. Abruptly she let the sail fall back to the ground and stepped off the board. She knew she had to put some physical distance between her and this man.

'That's enough for me for the time being,' she said, trying to keep her voice light. 'I think Emma's dying to get out on the water.'

Mac looked at her and the way his eyes danced told her he knew exactly why she had jumped off the board. His mouth twitched. 'Okay, then. Let's go, Emma.'

Abby found a rock and watched as Emma clambered onto the board and valiantly tried to pull the sail from the water. It took several attempts, but with Mac helping her she eventually got the sail up and started to move out towards the open sea. She must have surprised herself as she immediately let go of the sail and fell into the water. Even from a distance, Abby could see the flash of Mac's white teeth as he threw his head back and laughed. In response, Emma splashed him. Relief coursed through Abby. It really was the perfect way for Emma and Mac to get to know each other. From what she could see, the initial awkwardness of earlier had passed. It was early days, of course, but at least it was the right start.

After an hour, Abby was getting chilled despite having a cup of coffee from the flask she had packed. Emma had managed to get up on the board and move a little distance before falling off. Abby knew she must be getting tired and, sure enough, a few minutes later Emma and Mac, both grinning widely, made their way to shore. Emma flopped down beside Abby, her cheeks flushed and her eyes sparkling. 'That was so good.' She looked up at Mac, who was detaching the sail from the board. 'Can we do it again? Soon? Please?'

'Sure thing. But I think you should get changed now. I don't want you to get cold.'

As Emma hurried away to get dressed, Abby looked up at Mac. He really was gorgeous. No wonder Sara had fallen for him hook, line and sinker. She found herself wondering about him. How come a man as cute and as eligible as he was hadn't been snapped up? But perhaps he had. For all she knew, he had been married at one time.

'I think she enjoyed that,' Abby said.

Mac looked after Emma's retreating back. 'She could be very good, you know. She has natural balance and, more importantly perhaps, seems hugely determined to succeed. Is she like that in everything?'

Abby didn't attempt to hide her pride. 'She's a wonderful girl, Mac. She gives everything she does her best shot. I know her drive and determination will take her far in life.'

'And a lot of that must be down to the way you brought her up.' Mac's eyes glittered and once again Abby felt her body tingle in response.

'I hope so. But she has a lot of her mother in her, too.'

When Mac raised an eyebrow, a shot of anger coursed through Abby. She would not have this man making judgements about Sara. Okay, so Sara had been pretty wild, but she'd also been kind and loyal.

'Sara was a good person, Mac,' Abby said quietly.

Mac opened his mouth as if to reply but Emma, dressed in jeans and a thick woollen jumper, arrived back.

'Can we have something to eat now? I'm starving!'

The tension disappeared as they all laughed. 'It's not even ten o'clock yet, Em,' Abby protested.

'But it's ages since I had breakfast.'

'I swear I don't know where she puts it all,' Abby told Mac. 'She eats like a horse but is as thin as a rake.'

'At least she eats,' Mac said mildly. 'And she's still growing.'

'Mum says I'm going to be tall.' Emma looked shyly at Mac. 'I must take after you. How tall are you anyway?'

'Six foot three, or something like that. I'm hungry, too. What do you say we grab a burger?'

Abby frowned. 'I don't really like Emma to have junk food,' she said primly.

'I don't think one will hurt,' Mac protested.

Abby felt her hackles rise. One day as a father and already he was interfering. But she swallowed the angry words that rose to her lips. She was being overly sensitive. Why spoil the day by falling out over something as ridiculous as a burger? Nevertheless, she would have to speak to him and make it clear that as far as Emma was concerned, it *was she* who made the decisions.

'On the other hand,' Mac went on smoothly, 'there is a café up the road a little that does great home-made soup and sandwiches. And they have the best hot chocolate, too. Why don't we go there?'

'Whatever,' Emma said. 'I don't mind.'

Inside the café, Mac and Emma tucked into their soup and sandwiches while Abby nursed a mug of coffee.

She listened as Emma fired questions at Mac, and Mac replied with much the same answers he had given Abby. Nevertheless, there was a reticence, a carefulness about his replies that made her think he wasn't being totally candid. But why should he? No doubt he was, quite sensibly, feeling the way with his new-found daughter.

'Can I meet my grandmother?' Emma asked.

'Tiree is a long way from here,' Mac said evasively. 'But maybe one day.'

'Have you got brothers and sisters?'

'Only me, I'm afraid.'

Emma looked glum for a moment. Abby knew that part of her fantasy about finding her father was the hope that she'd discover a whole load of aunts, uncles and cousins at the same time.

But it wasn't long before her natural cheerfulness re-emerged.

'Did you always want to be a doctor?'

'For as long as I can remember,' Mac replied. 'What do you want to be when you grow up, or haven't you decided yet?'

'Not really decided. I might be a pilot or a vet.' She looked thoughtful. 'Or a doctor like you who rescues people. It looks fun.'

'Yeah, it can be fun, but it can also be a little scary at times.'

Emma's eyebrows shot up. 'I don't think you find anything scary.'

Oh, dear, Abby thought. One day in and already Emma had found a hero in Mac.

Mac flicked a glance at Abby and smiled. 'I find lots of things scary,' he said. Then he changed the subject. 'One of the other things I like doing is mountain biking. How do you fancy coming with me one day?'

'Oh, I'm not sure about that,' Abby interrupted before she could help herself. 'Can't that be pretty dangerous?'

Mac narrowed his eyes at her. 'It can be dangerous crossing the road, if you're not looking where you are going,' he said mildly. 'The important thing is to weigh up the risks, decide how you can best protect yourself then go for it.' Abby had the uneasy feeling he wasn't just talking about mountain biking. 'It's good for kids to test themselves. I believe it stops them from taking risks in other ways. Anyway, I'll only take Emma on gentle slopes and make sure she's wearing all the right gear to protect her.'

Once again he was challenging her authority as a mother and Abby didn't like it one bit. Keeping her voice level, she stood up. 'I'll think about it. Emma, it's time for us to get back. We need to go shopping for groceries.'

'Oh, do we have to?' Emma said. 'Can't I stay with Mac?'

Before Mac could say anything, Abby shook her head. 'I'm sure Mac has something planned for the rest of the day, and I would really like your help with the shopping, Em.' It was a pretty poor excuse, but Abby wanted Emma to get to know Mac slowly. Give them both time to let the relationship develop.

Reluctantly Emma got to her feet. 'Thanks, Mac. It was great.'

'We'll do it again next weekend, if you like,' Mac promised. 'And I'll try and work on Abby about the mountain biking thing.'

Emma smiled happily and Abby knew she was too late. Emma had found exactly the kind of father she had always wanted.

'Late night?' Kirsten teased. 'Some woman keeping you up?'

Abby caught her breath as an unfamiliar stab of jealousy hit her in the solar plexus.

Mac shook his head. 'I wish.' He smiled. 'No, I was called late yesterday afternoon. There was a nasty accident on one of the main roads. Two fatalities, I'm afraid.'

'But you saved one,' said Mike, who had walked in in time to hear the last of the conversation. 'I heard it was a real touch and go.'

Mac pulled his hand through his hair. 'I had to intubate at the scene. It wasn't easy, even with the fire brigade giving me some light to work with—and some shelter. The rain was pretty torrential. But, yes, the driver of the second car is going to be okay. I just wish we could have done something for the occupants of the other car, but it looks like they died on impact.'

Everyone hated hearing about death, even if they knew it came with the job. Abby was a little surprised to hear the sadness in Mac's voice. He usually gave away very little of himself.

'I ended up staying at the hospital until the small hours. I wanted to make sure before I left that the man pulled from the car was stable.'

He caught Abby's eye and smiled. 'I think it's important we follow up on our patients. Don't you, Abby?'

Abby smiled back. It seemed that Mac was breaking his no involvement rules in more ways than one.

Except with her, that was. He was always friendly when he collected and returned Emma.

'Anyway,' Mac said, 'back to work. Anything on the board?'

'Shouldn't you be at home, catching up on your sleep?' Abby asked.

Mac shrugged his shoulders. 'I'll be fine. We doctors learn very early on to do without sleep. A gallon of coffee and I'll be fine.' He must have noticed that Abby was far from convinced. 'Honest.' He held up two fingers. 'Scout's honour.'

While he'd been talking Abby had spooned some coffee into a mug and added water from the recently boiled kettle. 'Drink this,' she ordered.

As Mac sipped his coffee, the radio came to life and everyone stopped talking. They could only hear Kirsten's side of the conversation, but the look on her face told them it was a bad one.

'We have a pregnant woman who has gone off the road. The road ambulance and fire brigade are there, but they're requesting assistance from us. She's complaining of severe abdominal pain and they have no idea what they are dealing with. The fire brigade is cutting her out of her vehicle at the moment.'

Mac jumped to his feet, every trace of tiredness banished.

'Okay, Abby. Let's go.'

'Mac has called from the air ambulance. They are bringing in a pregnant woman from an RTA with severe abdominal pain,' Josh told the assembled A & E team. 'Would someone page the obstetric and paediatric registrar, please?'

'I'm on it,' the senior nurse said, turning away and picking up the phone.

Josh pulled a hand through his hair. He was tired. Spending so much time at the hospital, putting in extra hours, was taking its toll.

But you don't need to, an insistent voice whispered in the back of his mind. The department copes well when you're not there. He knew the real reason. It was more and more difficult to spend time at home with Rebecca, pretending. Some time soon he would have to face the reality of the situation, but for now it would have to wait.

Minutes later he was called to Resus to see his patient. Mac and Abby were by her side.

'Who have we got here?' he asked.

'Mrs Diane Clifford,' Mac replied calmly. 'Twenty-four weeks pregnant and has been having right-sided abdominal pain for the last six hours. She was driving herself to hospital when she blacked out and crashed. No obvious injury from the accident. We're going to have to leave you guys to it, I'm afraid. We have another call to go to.'

As Mac and Abby left, Josh smiled reassuringly as he palpated his anxious patient's abdomen. 'Don't worry, Diane. We'll get to the bottom of this.'

He glanced up as Megan swept into the room. As usual she looked every inch the calm professional, her dark hair neatly swept back from her face, her expressive eyes already taking in the scene.

'You called the paediatric registrar?' she said, acknowledging Josh with a faint smile before introducing herself to the woman on the bed. 'I'm Dr Phillips,' she said softly. 'We're going to get your baby attached to a monitor so we can monitor the heartbeat. Is that okay?'

Diane's frightened eyes darted from Josh to Megan.

'Do you think there's something wrong with my

baby?' She reached out and grabbed Megan's hand. 'Don't let me lose my baby.'

Pain flickered in Megan's eyes before she rearranged her expression into her usual professional mask. Anyone else would have missed it, but for Josh it was plain to see. Damn it. Why did it have to be Megan who was called to this particular case?

'Dr Phillips, could I have a word?' he said, indicating that Megan step outside the cubicle with him. 'Diane, the nurse is just going to get you attached to the monitor while I have a quick chat with Dr Phillips here. Is that okay?'

Diane nodded silently and Josh followed Megan outside the cubicle. They moved away so they weren't overheard by their patient.

'What are you thinking, Josh?' Megan's voice was calm and steady, but she couldn't quite hide the anxiety in her eyes. He knew her too well.

'It could be three or four things. Appendicitis, premature labour or an abruption. But I don't really believe it's appendicitis.'

Megan sucked in a breath.

'You could get someone else to take over,' Josh said gently.

Megan's eyes flashed. 'No, I couldn't. Josh, you have to stop treating me as if I were made of china. I'm here now and Diane is my case.'

'She's twenty-four weeks,' Josh continued. 'I hope to God we don't have to deliver her.'

Megan bit her lip. 'We both know a twenty-four-weeker doesn't have much of a chance. We'll give her steroids just in case. But if you need to deliver, we'll do the best for the baby.'

Josh wanted to reach out and touch her. The need

to comfort her was so strong he had to lock his hands behind his back.

'Okay. We'll do an ultrasound. See how the baby's doing when we get the CTG result. After that we'll make a decision. I'll give you a shout if we need you.'

But before he could turn away, Megan grabbed his arm.

'I'm staying,' she said. 'If she has an abruption you might have to deliver her without waiting for the obstetric team. But have a look at her ovaries. A cyst could present in much the same way.'

He nodded. He hoped she was right.

Everyone waited anxiously while Josh ran the ultrasound probe over the injured woman's abdomen. He looked up and smiled.

'There's a ten-centimetre cyst on the right where the pain is.' He caught Megan's eye. 'Good call, Dr Phillips. We were right to wait.'

They both knew they were far from out of the woods but at least it wasn't premature labour and it wasn't an abruption. It was still serious and Diane had to be taken to Theatre immediately. But at least this was one woman who wasn't going to lose her baby. Josh explained to Diane that the cyst had probably become twisted on its stalk, cutting off the blood supply to the ovary and resulting in severe pain.

Megan blinked rapidly. 'I better go and get changed. They'll need a paediatrician standing by in Theatre, just in case.'

Then she smiled. God, he loved her smile. It seemed to start somewhere deep inside her until her whole face lit up. Once more he felt a pang of regret so deep it hurt.

Why couldn't things have been different between them? How in God's name had he made such an almighty mess of his life?

CHAPTER ELEVEN

ABBY was surprised to find Mac waiting for her when she emerged from the building after changing into her civvies.

'Are you okay?' he asked, his eyes searching hers.

Abby nodded. 'I am now. It got a bit hairy there for a while. I always get really anxious when the victim is pregnant.'

Mac smiled slowly and his eyes creased at the corners. Abby's heart lurched. How could anyone look so cool and sexy after all they had just been through? She was sure she looked as if she'd done a couple of rounds in the boxing ring. It felt like it anyway.

For a moment Mac looked directly into her eyes and what she saw there made her heart start pounding again. The world started spinning around her.

'How about you and Emma coming out for dinner?' he asked.

Abby struggled to control her breathing. What she was feeling was nothing more than a delayed reaction to the rescue.

'Normally we'd love to, but Em is going around to a friend's after school. Maybe another time?' She was pleased to hear that her voice was steady, betraying nothing of her inner turmoil, and she thanked the years of practice she'd had of keeping her feelings hidden.

'We could go on our own.' He smiled at her. 'Go on, say yes. I don't know about you, but every time I go on a rescue, I get hungry.'

There wasn't any reason to refuse as far as she could see, except for her reluctance to be alone in his company a moment longer than she had to. Every time she was near him, her body kept behaving in the strangest way. On the other hand, what harm could it do? It wasn't as if she could avoid being alone with Mac for the rest of her life. Not when they worked together and not when they shared Emma. Emma would be having supper at her friend's and Abby had planned on warming up soup to have with a sandwich. She hardly saw her daughter these days. Emma was either going round to see friends, or staying on at school for hockey practice, or out with Mac. But although she missed spending time with her, she knew it meant her daughter was happy and settled. It was natural for Emma to want some independence, and it was a sign that she was continuing to develop her confidence, knowing that Mac and Abby were there if she needed them.

'Unless you'd like to have supper at my place?' she said. The moment the words were out of her mouth, she regretted them. Although the thought of an evening alone with Mac excited her, it unnerved her, too.

'Home cooking? How could I refuse?'

Too late. She could hardly retract the invitation now.

'It won't be very fancy, I'm afraid. You might regret it.'

'Let me tell you, Abby, for a man who lives on takeouts and microwave meals when I'm not eating out, the thought of home cooking is irresistible.'

'Okay, then, you're on. Why don't you come home with me now? It'll save you a trip to your flat and back.'

'Sure thing. I'll stop off on the way and pick us up some wine, shall I? Red or white?'

'White. Although I'm not much of a drinker, so you might be drinking most of it yourself.'

'Give me half an hour?'

By the time Mac knocked on the door, Abby had rummaged around in the fridge and found enough to make a stir-fry. As she'd told Mac, supper wouldn't be fancy, but with the soup it would be adequate. She hoped she had enough. A big man like Mac was bound to have a healthy appetite. Although there wasn't an inch of flab on his muscular frame, given all the exercise he did, he was bound to need calories.

'Wine—and some olives,' Mac said, proffering his purchases to Abby. 'I didn't know if you liked them, but I took a chance.'

'Love 'em. Why don't you pop the wine in the fridge? You don't fancy lighting the fire while I finish supper?' Abby gestured to the open fire with a nod of her head. 'You'll find everything you need there.'

By the time the meal was ready, the fire was burning cheerfully. There was no room in the tiny house for a kitchen table, so Abby set two places on the coffee table in front of the fire.

'Sorry,' she apologised. 'I guess it'll be slightly awkward for you, but as you can see there isn't a lot of space.'

Mac looked around the small sitting room-cum-kitchen.

'I don't know,' he said. 'It's kind of cosy. But you know, if you and Emma need something bigger, I'll be happy to chip in.'

'We manage fine,' Abby said, more sharply than she'd intended to. 'I'm looking for something bigger to buy once we're sure where we want to live.' She didn't add that it was nigh on impossible on her salary, but she guessed she didn't need to.

'It must have been a struggle sometimes, bringing up a child on your own,' Mac said quietly. 'I wish Sara had told me. I would have done something to help.'

Abby shrugged. 'If you knew Sara, you'd know she had her pride. I guess when she found out she was pregnant the baby was the first thing she'd ever had that was truly hers. All through her pregnancy she refused to tell me who the father was. She said it wasn't important. She only told me about you right at the end.' Despite her best efforts her voice cracked. Mac put his fork down and laid a hand over hers.

'Tell me about her. Although we spent those two weeks together, all I really knew about Sara was that she had a great sense of humour and a genuine love of life.'

Abby placed her knife and fork on her plate and leaned back on the sofa.

'To understand who Sara was you have to know something about our upbringing. Our mother—well, I guess you can say she wasn't the maternal type. When Sara and I were eighteen she told us it was time to leave home.'

'Go on,' Mac said quietly.

'I think my mother thought we got in the way of her

life. Men weren't that interested in a woman with two children.'

She sneaked a look at Mac and was surprised to see anger in his eyes.

He smiled but his eyes remained bleak. 'My mother was the same.'

'Sara and I set up home together, if you could call it that. We didn't have much money, but we got by.'

'What about your father?'

'We never really knew him. He left when we were three and didn't come back.'

'Like mine,' Mac muttered. 'Except he didn't wait until I was three. He was off the minute he knew my mother was pregnant.'

Abby's heart ached for him.

'Anyway, Sara went a little off the rails when we left home. It's like she thought she was unlovable, and who could blame her? If your own mother doesn't want you, what does that say about you?'

'And you? How did you feel?'

'I was different from Sara. I decided that it was my mother's problem and I would find a way of proving to her that I could make it on my own. All through our childhood, I was the responsible one.'

Abby picked up a cushion and clutched it to her chest. Despite her words she had been hurt by her mother's rejection. It still hurt. 'I trained as a paramedic. I dis-covered I was good at it. Sara, though, couldn't find anything she really wanted to do.' Abby blinked the tears away. She had tried everything to get her sister to believe in her own self-worth, but Sara just wouldn't—couldn't—believe it.

'When we were twenty-one I had saved up enough money to pay for a holiday in Mykonos for both of us.

I thought two weeks of sunshine, together, would bring us closer again. I had hoped that I could really talk to Sara. Convince her it was time she made something of her life.'

'And then she met me. I can't imagine you were best pleased.'

'Then she met you,' Abby said softly. 'I have never seen her so lit up. I think she fell in love with you the moment she set eyes on you.'

'She spent most of the holiday you had planned to-gether with me,' Mac said.

'Yes. It wasn't exactly the way I had thought it was going to be. But I couldn't deny her her chance. It had been a long time since I had seen her so happy.'

Mac groaned. 'I had no idea. I was so wrapped up in myself then, all I knew was that there was this beautiful woman who wanted to be with me. And I guess meeting me then falling pregnant was the last thing Sara needed. But how come I never noticed you?' He touched Abby briefly on her cheek. 'You are just as beautiful.'

'I wasn't back then. I was so much shyer than Sara. Anyway, the holiday wasn't a total disaster. I left Sara to it and took a ferry to the Greek mainland. I visited the Temple of Poseidon, and the Acropolis in Athens. Even if Sara had not been...' she paused '...occupied, she wouldn't have come with me. So I guess she got the holiday she wanted and I did, too. It was just a shame we didn't have the time I wanted to get closer to each other again.'

Abby smiled. 'I was happy for her. Those two weeks were the happiest I'd ever seen her. Instead of that vague sadness and emptiness that seemed to have followed her most of her life, it was as if she'd found something.

Something that made her believe in herself.' Abby looked at Mac. 'I know I have you to thank for that.'

'When did she tell you she was pregnant?'

'About three months after we returned from Mykonos. After we came back she was quieter, almost serene. I don't know…as if she'd found peace. I asked her if something had changed, but she just smiled. Then for a bit she was different again. Anxious and withdrawn. After a while, when she started showing, she told me she was going to have a baby. She said she hadn't told me at first because she hadn't been sure she was going to keep it.

'As you can imagine, I was stunned. I guessed the father must be you, but when I asked her she wouldn't say. She said it wasn't important. I didn't know how the three of us were going to cope, but Sara was so happy.'

Mac was listening intently.

'I wanted her to tell the father, even if she wouldn't tell me. I thought whoever it was had a right to know. But she refused point blank. She said the baby was hers and nobody was going to have any say about how she brought up her child. During her pregnancy she started a degree with the Open University. I could see she was determined to make a future for herself and the child and she knew I would always be there for her. Our own mother, of course, wasn't the slightest bit interested.'

'But she did tell you that I was the father— eventually.'

Abby squeezed her eyes closed.

'When she knew that she wasn't going to live to look after Emma, yes, she gave in and told me.'

The memory of those last few days were burnt into Abby's mind. At first everything had gone as planned and Sara's labour, although long, had resulted in a healthy baby girl. When Abby had seen her sister holding her child, it had been a moment of such joy Abby couldn't have felt prouder even if she had been the mother instead of Sara. Not even their mother's disinterest in the birth had blighted those first few days. After all, she and Sara had each other and however difficult and challenging the next few years would be, together they would be there for Emma, be their own little family. Then Sara had developed an infection and had been admitted to ITU. Even then, Abby had never suspected for one moment her sister might die. But Sara had got steadily worse. She hated thinking about it. Her sister, lying in ITU, pale and listless, and for once Abby had been totally unable to help her.

'Abby, I don't think I'm going to make it,' Sara had whispered, her face flushed with fever.

'Don't say that. Of course you're going to be okay.'

Sara smiled wanly. 'Somehow I knew deep inside that this was too good to last.'

Abby reached for her hand and squeezed it tight, trying to transfer all her strength to her failing sister.

'You can't die, Sara,' Abby cried. 'Emma needs you. I need you.'

'I'm not strong like you. You'll be okay.' For a moment strength returned. 'Look after Emma for me, promise. Don't let anything bad happen to her. I want her to know she's cherished and loved.'

'I promise, Sara. But you mustn't talk like that. You're going to be okay.'

'Hey, I thought I was the optimist.' Sara managed a smile. She struggled to speak. 'Remember Mac? Back on Mykonos? He's the father. I'll leave it to you to decide whether you want to tell him or not. Whatever you decide to do is okay with me.'

Shortly after, with Abby holding her hand, Sara had slipped into a coma. She never came round and died a few days later.

Tears fell as Abby repeated the story to Mac. She was barely conscious of his arm slipping around her shoulder and pulling her close.

'I'm so sorry,' he said. 'You must miss her. If I had known, I could have helped.'

'I tried to find you when Em was a few months old. But I knew nothing except that you were called Mac and taught windsurfing. I took Emma with me back to Mykonos to try and find you but the season was over and the resort closed down. I phoned their main office, but they refused to give me any details of the staff who worked there.' She shrugged. 'There was nothing more I could do, so we just came home.'

Suddenly conscious that she was in his arms, Abby pulled away. Her heart aching, she crossed to the fire and added a log. A sudden flurry of sparks crackled in the hearth.

'So you brought Emma up on your own. It couldn't have been easy. What about your mother?'

'She wasn't even there when Sara died. She had gone on holiday. Said she needed the break.' Abby couldn't keep the bitterness from her voice. 'To be fair, she couldn't have known Sara was going to die.'

'But you must have warned her? When Sara was admitted to ITU?' The anger in Mac's voice was almost palpable. How could anyone understand how a mother could stay away from her child when she needed her?

'She came back in time for the funeral,' Abby said. 'Then, unbelievably, when she held Emma for the first time, it was almost as if Mum changed before my eyes. She became besotted with her grandchild, in a way she never had been with her own daughters. Maybe it was different. There was no responsibility involved. She could have all the good times with Em without the bad. And maybe it was guilt. Guilt that she hadn't been there for Sara when she'd needed her most. Who knows? But she does love her granddaughter. She helped with child care when Emma was little so I could work. So people can change. And I'm glad. I've always felt it was important Emma knows who her family is. She's had little enough of them—until now, that is.' She forced a smile. 'But enough about that. What about your parents?'

This time it was Mac who shifted uneasily. 'My family isn't any better than yours, I'm afraid. If anything, they could be worse.'

Abby looked at him. He was studying his feet as if he could find answers there. She waited for him to continue.

'My mother sounds very much like yours. I also never knew my father. I sometimes wonder if my mother did. I was an only child and she made it clear from early on I was nothing but a nuisance.' He looked up and Abby saw the pain in his eyes. 'I spent as much time away from her as I could. She made it clear she didn't expect much from me, but I knew I wanted more from life. When I wasn't outside in the sea or on the hills, I was in my room studying. I was damned if I was going to give her the satisfaction of turning out the way she expected me to. I was lucky, I won a scholarship to medical school, and the rest is, as they say, history.'

'Do you see her?'

'I go back to Tiree once a year. She's not getting any younger. Whatever she is, she's still my mother.' He sent her a half-smile. 'You and I have a lot in common after all.'

'Does she know about Emma?'

'I phoned her. I thought she'd like to know. Perhaps she's mellowed or perhaps she's lonely, but she's asked to meet her.'

'Have you mentioned it to Emma?'

'I thought I should run it past you first.'

'Maybe we could all go?' Abby suggested.

'I'd like that.'

There was silence for a moment. 'I don't want Emma to grow up without a father. I told myself I would never have children, but now I have, I want her to know I'll always be there for her. Don't ever take her from me, Abby.'

Abby walked across the room and crouched by his side. She touched his face lightly.

'What makes you think I will? I want her to know her father, too.'

He touched her lips with a finger. 'Emma is lucky to have you as a mother.'

For a moment their faces were only inches apart. Abby could feel his breath on her skin, almost feel the warmth radiating from him. He smelled of wood smoke and earth. His eyes, drilling into hers, were as blue as the sea. Her heart was thudding so loudly she thought he must be able to hear it. Gently he slid his hand behind her neck. The feel of his fingers on her skin sent tiny shots of electricity fizzing through her.

She didn't know if he pulled her towards him or whether she was the one to make the move, but suddenly they were kissing. Softly at first, almost exploring each other's mouths, and then, as desire lit a flame in her belly, she was in his arms and he was kissing her as if his need for her was all-encompassing. No, no, no, a voice was shouting in her head. Don't do this. Nothing good can come of this. But her body wasn't listening. She could no more pull away from him than she could have walked across the desert.

Without knowing how it happened, they were lying on the sofa, their bodies pressed along the length of each other.

'Abby,' Mac whispered into her hair. 'Beautiful, sweet Abby.'

What was she doing? What were they doing? Apart from anything else, Emma would be back any moment. Reluctantly, Abby disentangled herself from Mac's arms and slid out of his grasp. Her heart was beating like a train and her breath was coming in short gasps. Mac reached for her again but she stepped away from his outstretched arm.

'This is so not a good idea,' she said.

'Why not? I think it's a very good idea.' His eyes darkened like the sea before a storm.

'Emma could come back any minute. I don't want her finding us in a clinch.'

'In a clinch?' The smile was back. 'Is that what you call it?' Laughter rippled under his words.

'Whatever.' Abby smoothed her hair with her hands. 'Nevertheless, if Emma walked in now...'

'Call it what you will, I think it's a very good idea.' He sat up and before she could move, his hand shot out lightning fast and caught her by the wrist, pulling her down on his lap. He buried his face in her neck, his lips touching her in places she hadn't even known, until now, had nerve endings.

She moaned softly. Being here with him felt so right. It had been so long since she'd been held. But she forced

herself to push him away. There was no way she could
think with him nibbling her neck.

'No, Mac. We can't. We have Emma to think
about.'

Mac frowned at her. 'Emma?'

'Yes. Can't you see? If we start something, it'll give
Emma all the wrong ideas. Besides, what if we fall out?'
She held up her hand to stop the words he was about to
say. 'It could happen, you know it could. How will it be
for Emma then?'

Mac's frown deepened. 'I wasn't really thinking of a
relationship. Hell, Abby, I wasn't really thinking at all.
You must know I find you attractive. What's wrong with
two adults…er…enjoying each other's company?'

Abby had to laugh. He was doing such a good imper-
sonation of a well-known, ageing movie star. 'Seriously.
Mac. Think about it. Don't we have enough to be getting on with? Trying to work out a way to co-parent
Emma?'

Mac drew his hand across his face in a gesture Abby
was beginning to know well. He looked so disappointed
Abby almost changed her mind. Almost.

Mac stood up. 'Perhaps you're right,' he said, reaching for his jacket. He stopped and looked at her intently.
'Right now, Abby, you're holding all the cards.'

And before she could ask him what he meant, the
door closed behind him with a gentle click.

CHAPTER TWELVE

BACK at his own house, Mac paced the floor. He still couldn't believe how much his life had changed in the last few weeks. It had been a shock finding out that he had a daughter, and the last thing he had expected was to feel the way he did about Emma. He found he was looking forward to spending time with her. She was so like him with her love of adventure.

And like Abby, too.

Over the last few weeks he had found himself drawn to Abby in a way that he had never been drawn to a woman before. It wasn't just that she was sexy, in that way that only a woman who had no idea of her own beauty could be, but it was her loyalty, her strength of character, her kindness that drew him. It couldn't have been easy bringing up a child—his child—on her own, but she had done it without a second thought. And she had made a good job of it.

But it was different now; he could help. Be there for Emma and Abby. Help financially. He thought about the little house they were renting. It was barely big enough for one, let alone two of them. And here he was in this spacious flat with more space than he knew what to do with. Perhaps he should ask them to move in with him?

Immediately he dismissed the idea. It was crazy. Abby

would never agree. The thought of sharing his home with Abby made the blood rush to his head. Seeing her every day. Her sleeping just a short distance away would drive him crazy. He'd never be able to keep his hands off her. And that way lay madness. She was right. What if they started something and it didn't work out? Having a child was one thing, but having a permanent relationship with a woman quite another. He didn't do relationships. If he started something with Abby it would, like all his other relationships, end sooner or later. And when it did there would be hard feelings and recriminations. There always were. No matter how often he warned the women in his life that he wasn't in it for the long haul, they never really believed him. They always thought they would be the one to change him. And if he gave in to his need to have Abby, what then? When it came to an end she might stop him from seeing Emma. He was surprised at how much the prospect alarmed him. Now he had got to know his daughter, he couldn't imagine a life without her.

And what if Abby met someone else? He didn't want that either. The thought of her in another man's arms made his blood boil. But if she did, what if she moved away and took Emma away from him? As it stood, he could do nothing to stop her. And what if that man treated Emma like his mother's boyfriends had treated him? As if she was a nuisance they could do without?

He pulled a hand through his hair. Now he had found Emma he was damned if he was going to let anyone take her away from him again.

The days sped by as winter approached. Abby kept her eyes open for a house for Emma and herself, but so far

nothing remotely affordable had come onto the market.
Abby knew the only realistic option for her and Emma
would be to buy something in serious need of refurbish-
ment, and she didn't have the time for that, or a small
modern flat, and she didn't have the heart for that.

Emma and Mac continued to spend time together
and had developed an easy teasing camaraderie. Often
they would gang up on Abby, once forcing her to join
them mountain biking. Although she had gone along
with them, one experience of being soaked to the skin
and terrified out of her mind had been enough. She had
refused point blank to go again. Some evenings Mac
would drop in and they would play Scrabble or play
games on Emma's computer console, the latter usually
causing Mac and Emma to share a laugh at Abby's ex-
pense. Abby didn't care. She treasured those evenings.
It was the family life she had never known.

One Saturday, Mac turned up at the cottage with a
big smile on his face. Although it was cold, the rain
had stopped and the sun was doing its best to cast some
sunshine their way.

'You're looking pleased with yourself,' Abby said as
she stood aside to let him in. 'But if you're looking for
Emma, I'm afraid she's gone into the town with some
friends from school.'

'It's not Emma I'm looking for. I have something I
want *you* to see.' His eyes were sparkling with barely
suppressed excitement.

'Oh, and what could that be?'

'I'm not saying. You have to come with me. Go on,
grab a jacket.'

Mystified, Abby did as she was told. Mac was waiting
for her in his Jeep.

'Where are we going? Come on, give me a clue.'

'No way. You're going to have to wait and see.'

They followed the road out of Penhally, heading in the general direction of St Piran's. But then Mac turned off and headed inland. A little while later, still refusing to answer Abby's questions, he turned up a steep track and came to a halt.

'We're here,' he said.

'Here? And where's here?' From where they were standing, Abby could see the coastline in the distance. Otherwise they were on a small bit of land surrounded by trees on the sides facing away from the sea.

'This little piece of land I'm standing on is for sale. Remember the boy we rescued from the bottom of the cliff? Dave, his father, came to see me. He wanted to thank us all personally. Anyway, to cut a long story short, it turns out he owns an estate agency here in Cornwall. I told him that I was looking for a small piece of land to buy and he mentioned that he knew of one that hadn't gone on the market yet. This one. Well, what do you think?'

'Think of what, exactly?'

'Of this as a place to build a house. As a home for you and Emma. You can't continue living where you are right now. And I know you haven't found somewhere to buy. So what about here? It's the perfect place to build a house.'

Abby touched him on the shoulder. She almost couldn't bear to destroy his excitement, but she had no choice.

'Mac, I couldn't possibly afford to buy this land, let alone build a house. It's a lovely idea, but completely out of the question.'

'I would bear the costs. After all, Emma is my daughter. You've met the financial costs of bringing her up on her own for years. Now it's my turn.'

Abby shook her head regretfully. 'I'm sorry, Mac. I couldn't possibly agree to it.'

His mouth tightened. 'Why not?'

'Don't you see? It's a wonderful, generous gesture, but I couldn't let us be beholden to you like that. It wouldn't be right.'

Mac's frown deepened. 'Beholden? Not right? Why don't you just come out with whatever it is you're trying to say?'

'Please understand, Mac. I've been independent all my life. I don't want to have to rely on anybody else. What happens if you meet someone you want to be with? Move away? Have a new family? What happens to us then? I'd never be able to meet the repayments on my own.' She shook her head. 'I'm sorry. I can't risk it.'

If it were possible, Mac's eyes turned an even darker blue. 'I have the right to make sure my daughter has as good a life as possible. You have no right to deny her because of some misplaced sense of pride. And what's more, I promise you, regardless of what happens in the future, I'll never abandon my child the way my father abandoned me.' His eyes narrowed. 'It is far more likely to be the other way around. You can up and leave with Emma any time you like, and I won't be able to stop you. How do you think that feels?'

Abby took a step towards him and touched him lightly on the arm. 'I wouldn't do that to Emma, or to you, Mac,' she said softly. 'Remember, I also know what it's like to grow up without a father. I would never deprive Emma of hers.'

Mac turned away and stood looking out to the horizon. This was a different side to Mac and her heart ached for him. But neither was she going to budge. He could be involved, she wanted him to be involved, but Emma was her responsibility and he had to understand that.

Mac swung around to face Abby. 'I want a DNA test,' he said abruptly.

Abby reeled. 'Why? I thought you believed me when I said you were Emma's father? Good grief, Mac, do you think I'm playing some kind of game here?'

He rubbed his face. 'I know you say now that you'll never take Em away from me, and I believe you mean it. But things change in life, Abby. I know that to my cost. People might mean to stick around, but in the end they don't.'

Abby started to protest but he cut her off. 'Besides, God forbid, what if something happened to you? What rights would I have then? At the moment, legally, you are her only blood relative. I wouldn't have a leg to stand on. A DNA test would prove I was the father to any court.'

What he was saying made sense, Abby admitted grudgingly. If she were in his shoes, would she take a chance that one day she might lose Emma? Absolutely not. She nodded.

'Okay. If, and only if, Emma agrees. The last thing I want is for her to think that you want the test for the wrong reasons. If you can persuade her, and if she's happy to have the test, I'll agree.'

The furrows between Mac's brow disappeared and he smiled. 'Thank you, Abby. That means a lot to me.'

They stood looking at each other for a long time. Mac took a step towards Abby, but before he could touch her, she turned away.

'Let's go home,' she said.

* * *

On the way back to her house, Abby thought about what Mac had said. Although she wanted Emma to have a relationship with a father who would be a permanent feature in her life, it felt as though everything was moving too fast. Mac wanted to be part of Emma's life and that was good. It would have broken Emma's heart if Mac had rejected her, but this... Wanting to have legal rights, wanting to contribute financially, it was more than Abby had anticipated. When she had told Mac about Emma, she had imagined a more casual relationship between father and daughter.

But now? He wanted more. And she couldn't blame him. And then there was this *thing* between her and Mac. Back then, she'd thought he was going to kiss her. And she'd wanted him to. But that would only make everything more complicated than it already was.

'Do you want to suggest the DNA test or shall I?' Mac asked.

'I think we should talk to her about it together,' Abby said. 'As soon as we get home.' She glanced across at him. 'She needs to know we're united about this, Mac.'

'At least we're agreed on something.' His expression was unreadable.

When they got back to the house, Mac suggested that they take a walk along the beach. Emma, as usual, was delighted to have any opportunity to spend time with her father. She particularly liked it when the three of them spent time together.

They stopped near some rocks and Abby poured hot chocolate from a flask she had brought.

'Em,' she started hesitantly. 'Mac and I have been talking.'

Emma looked at her warily. 'What about?'

'I think it's great that I've found you,' Mac said. 'As you know, I had no idea you existed until Abby told me. But now I want to make things more official.' He paused. 'I've got to kind of like having you as my daughter.'

A smile spread over Emma's face. 'And I kind of like having you as my father.' She threw herself at him and, wrapping her arms around him, squeezed him tightly.

The look in Mac's eyes made Abby catch her breath. The love for his daughter was there for anyone to see.

After a few minutes Emma released him and screwed up her eyes. 'How are things going to be more official? What do you mean?' She looked at Abby then at Mac. Her eyes lit up. 'Do you mean you two—?'

'No, Emma. You're way off there,' Abby interrupted quickly. Where on earth had Emma got that idea?

'I know it's not at all likely,' Mac said cautiously, 'but say anything happened to Abby, I'd want to have a legal claim on you. You know, make sure no one could take you away from me.'

Alarm flashed in Emma's eyes. 'There's nothing wrong with you, Mum, is there?' she said. 'You're not going to die or anything?'

Abby laughed. 'I have no intention of dying. At least, not for years and years. But, Emma, accidents do happen. What Mac is saying is that he's become very fond of you, and he wants everyone, particularly the courts, to recognise you as his daughter. Or rather him as your father. To do that you would both have to do a DNA test. Then if, and this is a big if, something happens to me, both Mac and I want to make sure you would get to stay with someone who loves you.'

Emma still looked anxious. Abby slid a glance at Mac. This was the last thing she wanted, Emma thinking they were hiding something from her.

Abby took Emma's hand in hers. 'I promise you, there is nothing wrong with me. If you don't want to have the test, that's fine. We'll find another way.'

'This test, is it like those they do in *CSI*?' Emma asked.

'Yes.'

'Will it hurt?'

'Not in the slightest. They'll take a swab from the inside of your mouth and do the same for Mac.'

Emma sat in silence for a little while.

'I don't mind, then. If you both think it's for the best.' She got to her feet and, finding a flat stone, turned to Mac. 'Can you make this skip on the water?' she asked. 'I can make it skip three times. Mum's record is four. Can you beat us?'

Abby and Mac shared a look of relief. Emma seemed reassured and what was even better, she was totally unconcerned about the test.

Mac took the stone from her hands. 'Four times, huh?' he said, grinning. 'I think I can do better than that.'

CHAPTER THIRTEEN

A FEW days later, Abby opened the door of her cottage to find Mac standing there. Her pulse stuttered disconcertingly. He was so damn good looking it just wasn't fair. But for once his easy confidence was absent. Instead, he looked ill at ease, almost embarrassed.

'Emma's out, I'm afraid,' she said. Anxiety rippled through her. He looked so serious. 'Is something wrong?'

'No,' Mac rushed to reassure her. 'It's just that I had an idea I wanted to run past you.'

Mac wanting to run something past her? That was a turn-up for the books.

'You'd better come in,' she said, standing aside to let him enter.

She signalled to him that he should sit, but Mac shook his head.

'Look, whatever it is, you'd better tell me.' Was this where he told her that the novelty of having a daughter was wearing off? Her heart rate upped another notch. If he let Emma down now, she'd throttle him.

'Remember you told me that Emma's birthday party had to be cancelled when nobody would come?'

Abby nodded. It had been almost the worst day of her life. It had been so cruel and so unbearable watching

Emma pretend it didn't matter. But Emma hadn't been able to hide the sobs coming from her bedroom later that evening. Abby had crept into bed with her daughter, holding her until the tears had subsided. That was when she had decided to leave London. She would never let her child be hurt like that again. Not as long as she had breath in her body.

'Well, I thought we should give her another party. Here. She's made friends now and perhaps it will take away some of the bad memories of London.'

Abby was so surprised she felt her jaw drop. It was the last thing she'd expected Mac to say. But she was touched and delighted and not a little ashamed. Once again, she had underestimated this man. As she looked at him her heart melted. He was a better man than he gave himself credit for.

'We could organise something really cool, like paintball or...I don't know...something else. We could arrange it all as a surprise.' Now that the words were out, there was no hiding his enthusiasm. 'I never had a party as a kid.' He smiled but he couldn't disguise the hurt in his eyes. 'I always wanted one, but my mother always refused. She said there was no way she was going to let a bunch of kids run riot in her house.'

'Me too,' Abby whispered. 'I would have given anything to be able to dress up in a party dress, just once. But my mum said parties weren't for the likes of us.'

They looked at each other and the world spun on its axis. Abby could hardly breathe. For a moment she thought he was going to pull her into his arms, but then he stepped back and let his arms to drop to his side.

What just happened there? Abby wondered. Her heart was racing as if she'd run up the highest hill in England. Every nerve cell in her body was zinging. Lord help her, she wanted him to have taken her in his arms. She wanted to lay her head against his chest, have his arms wrap around her, feel the pressure of his mouth against her. What was she thinking? Thinking that way spelled danger. He was so not the man for her. Why, then, did she feel this crushing sense of disappointment? Because she was in love with him. The realisation hit her like a ten-ton truck. She loved him and would do until the day she died.

'I think it's a great idea, Mac,' she said, turning away lest he read her discovery in her face. 'I can speak to the mums at the school, swear them to secrecy and get the invites out. We could organise it for the weekend. If we leave it any longer, someone's bound to give in to temptation and tell her. And I think the paintballing is a great idea. Emma's always wanted to have a go and the boys should enjoy it, too.' Hoping that she'd removed every trace of latent lust from her eyes, she turned back to him. 'I'm warning you, though, we'll both have to take part. You do know that, don't you?'

Mac grinned broadly. 'Why do you think I suggested it?' he said.

Emma was surprised but thrilled to find out about her party. Mac arrived before the partygoers and Emma flung herself at him, forgetting in her excitement to adopt the cool façade she had been trying to perfect lately.

'Isn't this the best idea?' she said. 'I can't wait for everyone to arrive so we can get started. Mum says she's going to join in, too.'

Mac looked at Abby over the top of Emma's head and grinned. 'I'm looking forward to seeing her moves,' he said.

Abby wagged a playful finger at him. 'Don't you underestimate me. I can run pretty fast when I have to.'

Emma's friends started to arrive, their laughter and shrieks of excitement filling the reception area. Mac had to shout above the clamour to make himself heard.

'Okay, guys. Before we get changed, we need to pick teams. Emma is captain of Team Arrows and, Simon, I believe you want to be captain of Team Blades. Since it's your party, Em, you get to pick first.'

Abby knew her daughter's every expression and she could see her hesitation as her eyes flicked between Abby and Mac. Abby's heart twisted painfully, sensing her torn loyalties. She wanted to choose Abby but also wanted to impress Mac. Was this how it was going to be from now on? She'd had her daughter all to herself for the past eleven years but now it was time to share her with someone else. Her father. Mac. The knot of jealousy felt alien to her but she had to remember this wasn't about her—it was about Emma.

Catching Emma's eye, she nodded her head slightly towards Mac. She caught the almost imperceptible flash of gratitude in her daughter's eyes as she selected Mac. Simon then chose Abby and the rest of the teams were quickly divided up.

Despite what she'd told Mac, Abby had no real idea what to expect. Obviously it had to do with firing balls of paint at each other and using various items around the course to hide behind to avoid being hit yourself. And taking the other team's flag.

When she emerged wearing her lurid green overall, she blushed under Mac's amused grin. She felt slightly ridiculous, holding her 'gun'. On the other hand, he looked the part in his blue overalls, like a dashing secret agent on a dangerous mission. The way he was looking at her warned her she was going to be his prime target. Abby felt a flutter of excitement—there was nothing she'd love better than to out-fox Mac. He was underestimating her if he thought she was Team Blade's weakest link! It was game on.

Fifteen minutes later Abby had to keep reminding herself it was only a game. The darkness, lit only sporadically by flashing lights and filled with atmospheric dry ice, heightened the tension and fun. Crouching behind a pillar, Abby paused to catch her breath. So far she'd managed to evade being shot, but so had Mac. Another flash of light and in that second she saw the top of his head behind a barrier. Abby crept forward, raising her gun slowly. Her finger tightened on the trigger and she stifled a giggle.

She didn't know how it happened but the next moment she was sprawled on her back with Mac's face inches from hers.

'Trying to sneak up on me, were you?' he growled into her ear. Abby could hear the triumph in his voice. She was distracted by the heat of his body on hers, his warm breath on her neck.

His eyes bored into hers. Her heart thumped against her ribs and she knew in that moment he was going to kiss her. Her lips parted involuntarily. At the very last moment, just before his mouth came down on hers, she wriggled out from underneath him. Despite being caught off guard, he moved much more quickly than she'd anticipated. Paint splattered from their respective guns until they were both covered from head to toe in myriad colours and laughing uncontrollably.

Grinning, Mac held out his hand. 'Truce?'

Abby took his proffered hand, only to let out a yelp of

surprise when he yanked her towards him. 'I believe you still owe me a kiss. And I intend to collect it...soon.'

It wasn't long before Emma's team triumphed, and after they had all cleaned up and changed they congregated in the café.

The children chattered happily about the game, arguing over their respective tactics.

Abby smiled at Mac, sitting opposite her at the table. 'Thanks for organising today. It's wonderful to see Emma looking so happy.'

'She's a fantastic kid. You have to take some of the credit for that.'

Abby glanced over at her daughter, her heart swelling with pride. 'Don't hurt her, Mac. I'll never forgive you if you do,' she said quietly. *And don't hurt me, she wanted to add*.

Mac shook his head. 'I've no intention of doing that.'

After they had cleaned up and the other children had left stuffed full of pizza and cake, Mac turned to Emma.

'The party isn't over yet,' he said. 'I've one more treat.'

Emma grinned at him. 'Tell me,' she implored.

'You have to come out to the car.' He led the way, a bemused Abby and Emma following in his footsteps.

'Close your eyes,' Mac told Emma. 'And no peeking.'

Emma did as she was told. Mac opened the boot of his Jeep and pulled out a board and something that looked like a kite. He placed them on the ground. 'Okay, you can open your eyes now, Emma.'

Emma's eyes grew wide. 'Is that what I think it is?'

'It's your very own kite-boarding stuff. In the spring, as soon as the weather is good enough, I'm going to teach you how to do it. You picked up windsurfing so quickly I'm sure we'll have you doing tricks with the kite board by the end of the summer.'

Emma turned to Mac and flung her arms around him. He picked her up and twirled her in the air. Abby's throat tightened. She knew this was Mac's way of telling them both he planned to stick around. When he deposited her back on the ground, Emma looked at him before hooking her arms into one of his and one of Abby's. 'This is the best day of my life,' she said.

Mac looked at Abby over the top of Emma's head.

'And mine,' he said quietly.

CHAPTER FOURTEEN

As DECEMBER approached, winter began to tighten its grip. The wind was sharper and the days shorter. Emma and Mac still went mountain biking and Abby rejoiced to see her child grow ever more confident, although she still fretted until Emma had returned home in one piece. The DNA results hadn't come back yet, but Abby wasn't surprised. They had been told that it could take months.

Mac and Emma arrived back just before darkness fell. They were both spattered with mud and their cheeks were flushed from the cold.

'I'm going to beat you one of these days,' Emma teased Mac.

'I hope you're not letting her go too fast,' Abby warned Mac. 'The last thing I want is to be involved in the rescue of you two.'

'Oh, Mum, you worry too much,' Emma complained. 'Dad would never let anything happen to me.'

A chill ran up Abby's spine and as she caught Mac's eye she knew he, too, realised the import of Emma's words. She was calling him Dad. If there was any doubt in either of their minds, she knew there was none in Emma's.

'Run upstairs and shower and change out of your wet clothes,' Abby told Emma. 'I'll get supper on.'

Mac still looked in shock as Emma left the room.

'Dad!' he said. 'She called me Dad.'

'So she did. How does it feel?'

'It feels strange. Very strange. But good. Yes. Very good.'

'Would you like to stay for supper, too?' Abby asked.

Mac grinned. 'I don't even want to sit down. In case you haven't noticed, I'm filthy.'

Abby had to laugh. Mac's face was almost black with thick dust. Only his eyes, where he had been wearing his goggles, were mud free. Impulsively she leaned forward and wiped his cheek with her finger.

His hand caught hers and he looked down at her with a glint in his eye. Her breath caught in her throat.

'Careful, Abby,' he warned. 'Don't start something you can't finish.'

She pulled her hand away as if she'd been stung. They stood staring at each other.

'Tell you what,' Mac said. 'Why don't I go home, get cleaned up, and I'll organise supper for the three of us?'

'I thought you didn't cook.'

'Didn't you notice I said *organise*? I didn't say anything about cooking. There is a great Chinese a few minutes' walk away from me. That's what I had in mind.'

'Emma is going to the cinema with a friend,' Abby said, looking at her watch. 'The mother is coming to collect her in an hour.'

'In that case, why don't you come? You could feed Emma and then come over. By that time I'll have cleaned myself up. You've never seen my place.'

'I don't know, Mac. Is it wise?' They both knew what she was talking about.

Mac took a lock of her hair between his fingers. 'I promise you, you'll be safe,' he said. 'It's just two work colleagues, friends, spending time together.'

Safe? What did he mean, safe? The flash of disappointment was unexpected. Was he implying that she wasn't his type? Perhaps she had misread him? Flirting came as naturally as breathing to men like Mac. He probably wasn't even aware he was doing it. She really needed to remember that.

'Or did you have something less innocent in mind?' he said.

She flushed. Damn the man. It was as if he could read her thoughts.

'Of course not,' she said coolly. 'You and I both know that.'

'So that's sorted, then. I'll see you around eight. Don't worry, I'll let you get back in plenty of time to be here for Em.'

'Okay,' she agreed finally, knowing she was risking her heart. 'I'll be there at eight.'

Mac smiled to himself as he drove home. Abby was much more transparent than she realised. He could read every thought and emotion that flitted across her face. She just couldn't pretend. That was what he loved about her.

Good God. Where had that come from? No way was he in love with Abby. Okay, he found her attractive, well, more than attractive, sexy as hell, and she was brave and funny and good and loyal and, damn it—he was in love with her. The shock almost made him collide with a car coming in the opposite direction. He pulled over to his own side of the road and the car passed him with a blare of its horn.

No! This was crazy. It was simply that he lusted after her. She was a challenge. The first woman he had ever wanted that hadn't fallen into his arms. But he knew he was lying to himself. He was in love. For the first time. And with Abby Stevens, the woman who was the mother of his child. So to speak. This wasn't at all what he had planned. He didn't do love. He didn't do for ever.

Mac was in all kinds of trouble.

Abby knocked on the door, thinking for the umpteenth time that she should have phoned and made her excuses. Was she stark, raving mad? Every bone in her body was telling her that it was a mistake to be alone with Mac.

Just as she was thinking of turning tail, he opened the door. Her breath caught in her throat. What a difference from the mud-splattered man of earlier. He had showered and changed into a dazzlingly white short-sleeved shirt and black jeans. Her heart rate went into overdrive. He looked divine. So confident and self-assured.

'Abby!' He smiled at her as if he had been waiting just for this moment and her legs turned to jelly.

'Hello, Mac.' Damn it. She sounded breathless. She cleared her throat. 'I'm not late, am I?'

'Bang on time,' he said. 'Our food should be here shortly. Come on in.'

He stood aside to let her pass and she squeezed past him, terrified lest she brush up against him. She could almost feel the waves of magnetism emanating from him.

'Let me take your coat.'

She almost yelped as she felt his warm hands brushing the back of her neck as he helped her shrug out of her coat. Little goose-bumps sprang up all over her body.

He tossed her coat onto the sofa. 'Can I get you something to drink?'

'Some sparkling water would be nice.'

His flat was the opposite from her little house in every way possible. Where her home had cramped, if cosy rooms, his was modern and open plan, with floor-to-ceiling windows looking out over the sea. Where her home was cluttered with the everyday minutiae that living with a teenager brought, his was sparsely but expensively furnished with enormous white sofas and bleached floorboards. On one side of the room there was a small kitchen with white units and a black granite worktop. It was fitted with every conceivable appliance down to an in-built coffee maker, she noted enviously. Not that it looked used.

In front of the sofas, which were arranged to form an L-shape, was a modern gas fire that looked almost real.

As Mac was pouring her drink, she wandered over to the ceiling-height book shelves opposite the windows. She found herself intensely curious to see what he read. Apart from several well-thumbed copies of the classics, there were thrillers and medical textbooks. She found herself smiling. There were few clues here about Mac. Was that intentional?

'One sparkling water,' Mac said, holding out a glass.

As she took it from him their fingers brushed and once again she felt a zap of electricity run down her spine.

'What do you think?' Mac waved his glass at the room.

'I like it.' Taking a sip of her water, she walked to the window and took in the view. Beneath her the lights twinkled and the moon, as bright and full as she could remember seeing, lit up the sea, so that she could see the waves rolling onto the shore. The windows where she was standing were actually a set of double doors leading out onto a small balcony.

'You can hear the surf from outside on a quiet night,' Mac said, coming to stand behind her. He was close enough for her to catch a faint smell of soap. 'It's one of the reasons I bought it.'

'I've always fancied a place with a view,' Abby said. 'Who wouldn't? But at the same time just having my own place with Em is good enough for me.'

'You really love her, don't you?'

'It would kill me if anything happened to her.'

'Why have you never married, Abby?'

The question startled her. She whirled round, taken aback to find herself within inches of his broad chest. She lifted her eyes to his, trying to ignore the blood rushing in her ears. 'I never met anyone who wanted me enough to take on a child, I guess,' she said softly. Then she grinned. 'Actually, that's not the whole truth. I've never met anyone that I thought I could live with, let alone marry. And the older I get, the more used to having my independence I get. What about you?' she challenged. 'Have you never met anyone you wanted to marry?'

'Me?' Mac laughed. 'I'm not into marriage, I'm afraid. I can't see the point. Why get married only to tear each other apart? It also implies that there is only one person for each of us and I don't believe that either. Unlike swans, I don't think humans are meant to mate for life.'

'What about children?'

Mac looked thoughtful. 'Having children was something I thought I would never do. What was the point? I liked my life exactly the way it was. But now...'

'But now...?' Abby prompted.

'But now I find I like being a father.' He turned away. 'Emma's amazing. I'm proud to be her dad.' He turned back to Abby and grinned. 'I never thought I'd say that, let alone mean it. And I have you to thank.' He crossed over to where Abby was standing. 'Thank you for letting me share her.' He touched her gently on the cheek and tipped her face so that she was forced to look him in the eye. 'I've had some of the best days of my life since I got to know her...and you.'

Abby's breath caught in her throat. Her heart was hammering against her chest. Slowly he lowered his head and, tipping her chin, brought his mouth down on hers. Abby had never felt sensations like the ones that were rocketing around her body. His lips were warm and hard, demanding a response from her. His tongue flicked against her and spurts of heat ricocheted from the tips of her toes to the top of her head. Her body felt as if it were on fire.

She couldn't resist him if her life depended on it. She could do nothing except give in to the feelings that were zipping around her. Her body melted into his as if it belonged there.

He groaned and, dropping his hands to her hips, pulled her against him. She fitted there in the circle of his arms as if once they had been one, and she let her hands go around his neck as she gave in to her need.

Still kissing her, he lifted her into his arms as if she weighed nothing and carried her out of the sitting room and into his bedroom. He laid her gently on the bed and she looked at him, knowing what was going to happen yet powerless to stop it.

His eyes were dark, almost hazy, as he looked at her. Without taking his eyes from her, he slid his hands up her hips and, hooking the top of her tights with his thumbs, he began to unroll them slowly. She lifted her hips to help him. Inside she was a mass of confusion. What little part of her brain that could still think was shouting, No! Don't do this! But the far greater part was taken over by urgent need of her body. She knew she was helpless to deny him...or herself.

The only light in the room came from the lounge and the moon outside. It was dark enough to hide her shyness but light enough for her to read every nuance of his expression.

Once her tights were off he turned his attention to her blouse. He leaned over and dropped kisses in the hollow of her throat, across her collarbone, his hands all the while deftly undoing her buttons. He stopped kissing her as he drew the blouse apart. He was breathing hard as he looked down at her. Now she felt no embarrassment, no shyness, only wonder at the expression in his eyes.

Then she lifted her hips as he unbuttoned her skirt and let it drop to the floor.

'You are beautiful,' he said, his voice thick with desire.

She hated him being away from her even for a second and she pulled him back towards her. As he kissed her, she let her hands slide under his T-shirt, revelling in the feel of hard muscle under her fingertips. How could a man who was so toned be soft at the same time? she wondered as she lifted his T-shirt over his head. She pressed against him, feeling the hard warmth of his bare skin pressing against her. She wanted him so much, she didn't know if she could wait a minute longer to feel him, all of him against her, inside her.

A small moan escaped her lips as she searched for the button of his jeans, her fingers brushing the hair that travelled from his belly downwards.

This time it was him who was helping her as his jeans came off.

Then he stretched on the bed beside her. She blushed when she saw the extent of his desire for her.

He slipped a thumb inside the cup of her bra, teasing one nipple and then the other, until she didn't know how she could bear it.

Then his hand reached behind her, deftly unhooked her bra and her breasts sprang free.

He kissed her skin, running his tongue across each nipple. Her body was on fire. She couldn't wait any longer. She was going to explode.

'Please,' she whispered. 'I can't hold on...'

'Just a little longer,' he promised. 'But this time, our first time, I want to watch you.'

She shook her head from side to side. She wanted him inside her now. Moving with her. Filling this empty, aching void that she hadn't known, until now, existed.

'Shh,' he said. 'I promise you there will be time later.'

Giving in, she lay back, digging her fingers into his hair, curling her fingers tightly in an attempt to stop herself crying out as he inched his mouth downwards.

Dropping kisses on her belly, on the insides of her thighs, brushing his fingers gently between her legs. Then he removed her panties and just when she thought she couldn't bear the exquisite pain of her need any longer, he slipped his finger inside her. He raised his head and looked deeply into her eyes as she arched her body up to him. She couldn't help the cry that ripped from her throat as sensation after sensation rocked through her body. He was taking her somewhere she'd never been before, higher and higher, until at the top her body couldn't hold on any longer and she lost all sense of who she was.

Her head was still reeling as she clutched him to her. She needed him inside her, and greedily she pulled him on top of her, opening herself to him and using her hands to guide him inside her. They rocked together, more and more urgently, until triumphantly she heard him reach his climax, just seconds before she followed him.

They lay, breathing deeply, their bodies hot and entangled. She felt as if every cell in her body had merged with his. She had never known sex could be like this, a heady mix of the physical and emotional. His hands were brushing over her hair. Lightly touching her shoulder.

'My God, you're not nearly as prim and proper as you appear on the outside, are you?'

She blushed, but hearing the laughter in his voice she couldn't take offence.

'I haven't had many lovers,' she murmured.

He propped his head on his elbow as he looked down at her. 'I'm glad,' he said simply.

His hand trailed lazily over her neck and then onto her breasts and her breath began to quicken. 'I don't want to think of you being with anyone else,' he said possessively. 'I want you to be mine. Just mine.'

Her heart started its hammering again. She was surprised he couldn't feel it pounding against his hand as he continued to touch her body, searching for the spots that drove her wild. Didn't he realise that wherever he touched her drove her wild? Her last coherent thought as she succumbed once more to the relentless demands of his touch was that she loved him. Loved him, completely, irrevocably and for ever. Before she could help herself the words slipped out. 'I love you,' she whispered as he once more took possession of her, body and soul.

Mac lay listening to the gentle sound of Abby's breathing. Her hair was fanned out across his chest and he swore he could smell strawberries. It felt so right to have her curled up against him—right and peaceful.

As he began to drift off towards sleep, an image of Abby, Emma and himself came into his head. They were laughing together as they shared a meal around the table in Abby's kitchen. Abby and Emma were looking at him with such love and admiration it made him feel good. Better than he had felt in his life. But then he started. What had Abby said? She loved him. He knew women often said that in the throes of making love. They didn't necessarily mean it. He groaned quietly. But Abby wasn't any woman. She was strong and proud and honest. She wouldn't have said the words if she didn't mean them.

There was no chance of him falling asleep now. His mind was racing too fast for that. Gently he disentangled himself from Abby and eased himself out of bed. He wrapped a towel around his hips and crept out of the bedroom and into the sitting room. He opened the door to his small balcony and stepped outside into the cold air. Maybe it would knock some sense into him. He had been a crazy, selfish fool to let it get this far. He should have known better than to play with Abby. But he hadn't been able to help himself. Ever since she'd appeared back in his life, his need to take her to bed had been like an itch he'd needed to scratch. But he hadn't been thinking of her. What could he offer her? It was one thing to accept the responsibility of a child—there was nothing he could do about that, he had a duty towards Emma—but a relationship with Abby was out of the question. He hadn't changed his mind about not wanting commitment. Commitments brought trouble and pain. Commitments were not for him. Even if he loved her.

He heard the pad of feet behind him and two soft hands crept around his waist.

'What are you doing out here in the freezing cold?' Abby asked, laying her cheek against his back. Her silky hair was like a caress against his skin, and despite everything he had just been telling himself he wanted her there, always.

Suddenly she moved away from him and he felt it like a stab to his heart. He had to tell her what he felt before either of them got in any deeper.

'It can't be ten o'clock. Grief, Emma's due back at half past. I have to get home.' She had wrapped a sheet around her before coming onto the balcony and almost tripped over it in her haste to get back to her clothes in the bedroom. He smiled at her ungainly, faltering steps and had to force himself to stay where he was. If he touched her again, he'd be undone.

'My shoes—where are my shoes?' Abby's panicked voice came from the bedroom. She had slipped on her skirt and blouse and rammed her tights haphazardly into her bag.

'Hey, slow down. It'll only take you fifteen minutes to get home. Plenty of time.' He retrieved one of her high heels from under the sofa and the other from the floor halfway to the bedroom. 'Your shoes, milady,' he said.

She practically snatched them from his hands. 'It's

no laughing matter,' she said crossly. 'I've never not been there for Emma when she comes home. She'll be anxious. And anything could happen. There might be a fire. She could get trapped. Hurt herself and need me. What was I thinking, falling asleep?'

She put her shoes on and looked around feverishly. Mac picked up her coat from the arm of the sofa and held it out so she could slip her arms into it.

'C'mon, Abby. You know nothing's going to happen to her in the few minutes she'll be alone. It's just that you've been on too many rescues. That's why you're imagining the worst.'

She glared at him. 'Being a parent brings responsibility, too, Mac. And one of those responsibilities is protecting your child from any danger.'

Mac knew it was useless to argue. Besides, which would he rather? The woman who was mother to his child caring too much or caring too little? He groaned inwardly. Wasn't that the problem? Abby was the kind of woman who would always care too much. And he didn't want or deserve that.

He was aware of her lips brushing his, and then she was gone.

Happily, Emma hadn't got back by the time Abby brought her car to a screeching halt outside her little house. Everything was still in darkness. Mac was right. She had overreacted. But if anything should ever happen to Emma, she would simply die.

As she let herself in, she thought back over the evening. It had been the most exciting night of her life. A delicious thrill ran up her spine as she recalled how it had felt to be in his arms. She had never imagined that making love could be like that. Although she'd had lovers in her life before, neither of them had made her feel like that. Was it because she loved Mac? The thought frightened and excited her at the same time and she grew hot as she remembered how she hadn't been able to stop herself murmuring the truth to him.

She ran upstairs and switched on the shower. It would give her time to regain her composure before facing Emma. As she let the hot water stream over her body, she pushed aside the memory of Mac's hands. She could have sworn he wasn't immune to her. But then again, what did she really know about men?

He didn't say he loved you. The voice wouldn't go away. But that was okay. For the first time in her life she was going to throw caution to the wind and let life take her where it would. If there was one thing being with Mac had taught her, it was that life was nothing at all if you didn't take risks.

Nevertheless, she was still hurt and dismayed when over the next few days Mac was friendly but distant towards her. Although she hadn't expected protestations of undying love, neither had she expected to be treated like a one-night stand. Had she flung herself at him? Now that he had slept with her, was he no longer interested? He still spent time with Emma on a regular basis, but his invites no longer included her. It was becoming evident she had made a dreadful mistake. But one she could not regret. Making love with Mac, loving Mac, had made her feel alive. And if part of that was the dreadful pain of rejection she knew deep down that she accepted that, too. At least Emma had a father who loved and cherished her. That would have to do.

CHAPTER FIFTEEN

IT WAS another Saturday when Rebecca was on her own. Josh had gone to work, telling her that he had loads of paperwork to catch up on. Although he had promised to be back soon after lunch, it was almost three and he still hadn't returned. It was typical of Josh. In the four years they had been married she had grown to accept that his work would always take priority over her.

A few days earlier she had brought up the subject of children again. Josh had refused to even discuss it and they had argued. Since then they had been barely speaking. Josh was spending more and more time at the hospital and Rebecca had the distinct feeling that he was avoiding her.

She packed a sandwich and a flask of coffee. Josh hated hospital food. They could take their picnic and despite the cold, maybe they could find a bench and sit outside and talk. She blinked away the tears. When had they last talked properly? She couldn't remember.

As she drove towards the hospital she suddenly felt nervous. She could hardly blame Josh totally for the gulf in their marriage. She could make more of an effort, take an interest in his work, even if it did bore her senseless. She would suggest they go into London for dinner, meet up with old friends. It would be like it had been in the beginning. Her spirits lifted. Perhaps they could still find their way back to each other and then if they did, Josh might agree to have children. She would make him see that a baby would make them happy again.

She turned into the hospital car park and searched for a parking place. Then she rooted around in the back seat of her car until she found the paper bag with the picnic. Once again she checked her make-up and her hair. Was that a frown line between her eyes? She shivered. Every day she was seeing signs that she was getting older.

She hopped out of the car and took a few steps towards the door of A & E. But then, to her left, sitting on a bench under a tree, she saw them. Josh and another woman. Like Josh, the other woman was wearing scrubs, and although her hair was pulled back in a ponytail and her face was devoid of make-up, she was still startlingly beautiful in the way only certain women could be. Rebecca felt a flash of envy. She knew she was beautiful, too, but she needed the help of make-up. She didn't have the natural beauty of the woman sitting next to Josh.

She was about to call out when she froze in her tracks. Josh threw back his head and laughed at something the woman had said. His arm was draped over the back of the bench, almost touching her shoulder. There was a familiarity about the gesture that spoke volumes. Rebecca couldn't tear her eyes away. When had she last heard Josh laugh? When had she last seen him looking so relaxed, as if he didn't have a care in the world? When had she last seen him look *happy*?

The woman raised her face to Josh's and smiled into his eyes. Rebecca's throat ached and she raised her hand to brush away the tears that stung her eyes. Slowly she backed away, terrified now lest they see her. Although she couldn't bear it, she knew. Knew with a certainty that rocked her soul. Josh was in love with this woman. Rebecca could see it in every line of his body, in the way it seemed as if she were something precious he had to protect.

Tears were blinding her as she groped her way back to the car. Whatever she'd had planned, whatever hopes she'd had for her and Josh making a go of their marriage, it was too late. If Josh loved this woman, he would be with her. He was too honest to continue with a marriage when he was in love with someone else. Anger was beginning to erode some of the pain. How could she have been so stupid not to have seen what was in front of her eyes? It wasn't work that was making Josh spend all these extra hours at the hospital, it was another woman.

Rebecca gripped the steering-wheel with numb hands. He would leave her. Maybe not today, or tomorrow, but soon. He would look after her financially, she knew that, but leave her he would. And all these years she had stayed with him—giving up her dream, her longing to have a baby, giving up her happy life in London to follow him here, to a place she knew she could never be happy—had been futile.

She turned the key in the ignition. She was damned if she was going to walk away with nothing. At the very least she would have a baby to love.

The telephone was ringing as Mac stepped in to his flat after playing squash. At first he didn't recognise the voice.

'Mac? Robert here.' Mac stood still. He had almost forgotten about the doctor in charge of doing the DNA test.

'Hello, Robert. How's it going? Have you news for me?' Too impatient for small talk, he cut to the chase. He knew it was ridiculous but suddenly he was nervous.

Robert cleared his throat. 'I do. You'll get a letter confirming the results tomorrow, as will the other party, but I thought as a professional courtesy I would ring you.'

Get on with it, Mac wanted to shout down the phone, but he held himself in check. Robert could have left him to find out by letter.

'And?'

'I'm not sure if it's good news or bad, but…'

If he could have reached down the telephone line and shaken Robert he would have done so. Why didn't the man just get on with confirming that Emma was his child? As soon as he had the proof, he would ring the lawyer and start the proceedings that would allow him to be named officially as Emma's father.

'The test is negative,' Robert said flatly. 'There is no way at all she could be your child.'

The breath came out of him like an explosion. He hadn't been even aware he had stopped breathing.

'What?' he managed. He couldn't have heard right.

'Emma Stevens is not your biological daughter. As I said, I have no idea whether this is good or bad news, but that is the result. A letter is on its way to her guardian.'

Mac felt the world tip. Emma was not his daughter. He couldn't believe it. Everything in him said she was. He couldn't love her the way he did if she wasn't his flesh and blood.

He was hardly aware of thanking Robert and replacing the receiver. If it hadn't been mid-afternoon, he would have poured himself a stiff whisky.

Emma wasn't his child. Sara had either been lying or, he suspected, simply mistaken.

He was surprised at how devastated he felt at the news. What now? Would Abby stop him from seeing Emma? The thought made his stomach churn. Now he was about to lose her, he realised how much he had begun to enjoy the role of father.

And what about Emma? His heart ached for the little girl. She cared deeply about him. He knew that. How would she feel when she found out that he wasn't her father after all? He raked a hand through his hair. God, it was such a mess. Why hadn't he seen this coming? Why hadn't he reminded himself that there was always a possibility that the test would be negative?

But he knew the answer. Bit by bit he had fallen in love with the idea of being a father. He had enjoyed being around for Emma. Encouraging her to come out of her shell. All the things his father should have done for him, but hadn't. In some ways, he had been able to give Emma some of the childhood pleasures he'd never had, and it had healed something inside him.

Making up his mind, he picked up his jacket from where he'd flung it and was out of the door. He had to speak to Abby. She would know what to do.

Abby paced her small sitting room. Where was Emma? She'd promised she'd be back for lunch and it was now after one.

She picked up a magazine and attempted to read it, but there was no way she could concentrate. Emma knew Abby worried. She would have texted her had she been held up.

She had wheedled Abby into agreeing that she could go down to the beach with a friend from school. Simon was a local boy and knew the area well, so why was she worrying? They were going to go down to the beach and stop off for a burger. But Emma had promised she'd come home after that. Abby checked her watch for the hundredth time. Only five more minutes had passed, although it felt like a lot longer.

She almost jumped out of her skin when her mobile rang. She leaped on top of it. It was bound to be Emma, probably apologising for not being home, for forgetting the time.

And it was Emma. At least, she thought it was. The signal kept fading and all she could hear were muffled snatches of words.

'Em? Is that you? I can't hear you. Can you go somewhere where you can get a better signal?'

'No...stuck...help...'

Abby's blood ran cold. She could hardly make out the words but there was no mistaking the fear in Emma's voice.

'Em? Where are you?'

More static. Then three words that made her physically ill. 'Trapped...cave...tide...' Then all of a sudden Emma's voice came over clearly. 'Help us, Mum.'

Her daughter, her beloved Emma, was in trouble. Abby forced back the waves of terror that threatened to overwhelm her.

'Stay calm, Emma, and tell me where you are.'

'Cave...beach...hurt...'

'Are you hurt? God, Emma!'

But there was only more static on the end of the phone. 'Look, Emma, I don't know if you can hear me, but leave your phone on. I'll find you. I promise. Keep calm, I'm coming.'

'No time... Hurry—' And then the phone cut out.

Abby was almost sobbing with terror. She had to find Emma. But where to start?

For a second she couldn't think what to do, and then suddenly the door opened and he was there. Mac! Relief made her knees go weak.

'I knocked,' Mac started to apologise, but the expression on her face must have told him something terrible had happened. He was by her side in seconds, pulling her close. 'Breathe, Abby. That's it. Slow, deep breaths, and tell me what's happened.'

This was wasting time! She pushed him away.

'It's Em. She phoned. Just now. I couldn't hear properly. Just enough... Oh, my God. I have to go to her.'

Mac reached out for her and pulled her round to face him. His face had lost all colour and his eyes were as dark as ink.

'Tell me,' he said.

'She's trapped. And hurt. She needs us, Mac,' Abby moaned. 'Help me, find my baby. Our child. Please, Mac. You have to help me.'

'Listen to me.' He grabbed her by the shoulders. 'Look at me, Abby.'

She looked into his eyes. She saw fear and something else. Conviction.

'We're going to find our girl. Do you hear me? And she's going to be all right. But I need you to tell me everything.'

'She went to the beach with a boy from her class. Simon. That was almost three hours ago. She said she'd be back by one. She promised.' She took a gulp of air. Mac was right. Panicking now wouldn't help Emma. 'She phoned. The signal was bad. I could hardly hear her. All I could make out was that she was trapped. In a cave. And hurt.' She took a shuddering breath as terror returned. Her baby. Out there somewhere. Alone and scared.

Mac was already on his phone. 'I'm going to alert the rescue services. We need to get the coastguard and the other services out looking.' Abby paced as he spoke into the phone for a few minutes. All she could hear was Mac's side of the conversation, repeating what she had told him. When he finished the call, he looked grimmer than ever.

'What is it?' Abby asked. 'What did they say?'

'They said they'd mobilise a sea and air rescue,' Mac said. But Abby could tell there was something more. Something he wasn't telling her.

'Tell me everything they said.' She kept her voice level. 'I have a right to know.'

He hesitated.

'Please, Mac, tell me.'

'The tide is coming in,' he said. 'And it's higher than usual today. If they are trapped somewhere, it's only going to get worse.'

Abby cried out and sank to her knees. In a flash Mac was by her side. He lifted her into his arms and held her tight before placing her on the sofa.

'You stay here, Abby. In case Emma phones. Keep trying her mobile. I've got to go.'

Abby struggled to her feet. 'I'm coming, too.'

'It'll be best if you don't.'

'Don't even think of trying to stop me,' she said. She took a deep shuddering breath. 'I'll be okay. I promise. I won't panic and I won't get in the way. But I'm coming.'

Five minutes later they were prowling the cliffs above the beach front. Mac had managed to get hold of Simon's parents. They were also panic-stricken but had told them of a cave that Simon liked to explore. They told Mac that they had forbidden their son from going into the cave, but suspected that he, trying to impress his new friend, might have ignored their warnings. The cave was easily accessible when the tide was out but, depending on the size of the tide, could become filled with water, preventing escape. Instinctively Abby knew that this was where Emma was. At the very least they had nowhere else to try. When it arrived, the Royal Navy helicopter would keep searching from the air and the coastguard would search the shoreline.

As soon as Abby and Mac got the information about the cave, they ran towards the part of the beach where it was. Although Abby knew the tide was rising, she couldn't help a small cry when she saw that the beach had completely disappeared under the sea.

How would they get to the stranded children, and even if they did find them, how would they get them out?

'We need divers,' Mac was speaking into his mobile. 'The navy will have them. Get them down here immediately.'

Divers! If they needed divers to get to the children, they were in deep trouble. It would take time to get them here. And time was what they didn't have. With every minute, the tide was rising higher.

Mac ran into a shop selling gear for watersports. He returned a few minutes later with flippers. The kind divers used. 'I can move much faster with these. Try and get Emma again,' Mac said. 'Even if you can't hear her, she might be able to hear you. Tell her help is on the way. Try texting her, too. Sometimes a text will get through even if a call won't.' Uncaring of who might be watching, Mac stripped off his clothes until he was down to his boxers and T-shirt. Tossing his clothes to one side, he pulled on the flippers.

While he was doing that, Abby tried Emma's mobile again, despairing. She had tried every minute or two since she had got Emma's call, but it was hopeless. Her fingers fumbling with the tiny buttons, she sent a text.

Coming for you. Dad is here. Hold on. We love you.

As she pressed 'Send', Mac declared he was ready.

'We don't have time to wait for the rescue services. I'm going to go down there now. As soon as the Sea King gets here, make sure they know exactly which cave I'm searching. The coastguard, too. They'll have a pretty good idea of where the cave mouth is. The air ambulance is on its way with Lucy and Mike.'

He looked down at her and gently raised her chin, forcing her to look at him. 'I'm going to get her, Abby. I promise you. She'll be home safe with you soon.'

'Isn't it better to leave it to the Navy divers?' she had to ask.

Mac shook his head. 'She might be hurt. Or him. Or both. They may need medical attention. It has to be me.'

Abby nodded. Despite her terror, she knew Mac would do everything in his power to save their child, even if it meant sacrificing his own life. The thought of losing him, too, rocked her soul.

Just as he had done those weeks before, Mac disappeared over the side of the cliff. But this time the stakes were higher.

The water was freezing and murky. Mac forced himself to wait a minute or two to let the water settle. He had to be methodical and not let his impatience to get to Emma and her friend cloud his judgement. As he had hoped, after a few agonising seconds the water cleared and he was able to see the entrance to the cave. There was still a gap between the mouth of the cave and the sea, but Mac knew it wouldn't be long before that small opening disappeared.

He used his fins to propel himself towards the cave. The tide was so high. Would he be rescuing two corpses? No! Thinking like that did no one any good. He had to believe that Emma and her friend had found a high ledge to wait on.

He swam underwater towards the cave opening. After a few metres he stopped and raised his head to get his bearings. He was in a cave that stretched a metre above his head. It was almost completely dark inside and Mac had to strain to see anything. Damn it!

'Emma!' he shouted, his voice echoing in the semi-darkness. His heart plummeted when there was no reply. Had they got it completely wrong and were searching in the wrong spot? Or, even worse, was it too late?

He heard a noise coming from his right. He whirled round, trying frantically to make out in the gloom where the noise had come from. Then he saw them. Two small figures huddled together on a ledge. Relief coursed through him, to be replaced almost instantly by anxiety. They were still in desperate danger. The rising tide was lapping at their feet.

'I'm coming,' he yelled, frantically searching for another ledge. A higher one, where the tide couldn't reach. But there wasn't one. He had to get the children out. But how?

Quickly he swam towards the children.

'Hey, there,' he said softly. 'How're you doing?' He knew the children would be very frightened.

'Dad!' It was Emma's voice, Mac noted. Whatever injuries she might have, at least she was conscious. 'You found us. See, Simon? I told you my dad would find us. He rescues people all the time.'

The irony wasn't lost on Mac. The first time she really needed him was the day he'd found out that he wasn't her father. But that didn't change the way he felt. Not one iota. He couldn't love Emma any more if she were his biological child.

'Dad. Simon's hurt his leg. We think it's broken. That's why we couldn't get out. When the tide started coming in we managed to get up here, but we couldn't go any further.'

And you didn't think of leaving your friend and saving yourself? My brave, darling child. She was so much his and Abby's child, whatever the DNA test said.

Mac heaved himself out of the water and onto the ledge beside the children. There wasn't much space. A quick examination of Simon's leg told him Emma was right. It was broken. And not just broken—the boy had a compound fracture and was bleeding badly. The loss of blood, combined with the cold and fright, was having a bad effect on the young lad. He was shivering uncontrollably. They had to get him to hospital, and soon.

'I'm going to strap your leg as best I can,' he told the boy, 'and then I'm going to get you out of here, okay?' As he spoke he struggled out of his soaking wet T-shirt. It wasn't a great bandage, but it was all he had.

'I'm sorry, but this will hurt a little,' he told Simon. He straightened the leg as best he could before strapping it with his T-shirt.

'Emma, I'm going to have to take you out of here one at a time, do you understand? And I'm going to have to take Simon first. He's the one in need of help most urgently.'

It broke his heart to see the fear then resolve on Emma's face. She lifted her chin. 'That's okay,' she said. 'I can wait.'

He was so proud of her. Any other child would be crying, but not his Emma.

'Abby is waiting for you outside.'

He explained to Simon what he wanted him to do. 'Lie on your back and don't, whatever you do, try and fight me. I'm going to put my hands on either side of your head, and pull you out. As long as you don't panic, you'll be fine.' There was just a big enough gap between the top of the entrance to the cave and the water for him to make it out with the boy. But would there still be a gap by the time he returned?

Mac was facing the worst dilemma of his life. How could he leave Emma? What if he didn't make it back in time? How would he live without Emma? How would Abby live without the child she loved?

But if he had any chance of saving Emma, he had to act now.

'I'll be back as quick as I can,' he said. 'Hold on.'

He grasped Simon around the head and pulled him out of the cave, taking care not to let water splash in the boy's mouth. If the boy panicked now, it could be fatal for both of them. As he swam, his heart and soul was back in the cave.

He found the rock where Abby was still waiting. She had been joined by the crew of the air ambulance. Lucy and Mike were standing by, waiting to help him. From the corner of his eye he could see the lifeboat circling nearby. He knew they couldn't risk getting any closer. There was no sign of the Sea King. It must still be waiting for the divers.

'Where's Em?' Abby's face was white.

'She's still in the cave. I'm going back for her. I couldn't take her as well as Simon.'

Mac was helping Lucy and Mike carefully lift Simon out of the water and onto a stretcher. Before he could stop her, Abby jumped into the water and was swimming towards the entrance of the cave.

'No, Abby, wait!' he shouted, but either she couldn't hear him or she was ignoring him. She carried on swimming towards the cave.

Muttering a curse, Mac gave one final heave and his arms lightened as the injured boy was taken out of his arms. He plunged back into the water after Abby. Didn't she know that she, too, could drown? He could lose both the people he loved most in the world. The realisation cut through his fear. He loved Abby. He loved her more than his life itself. He had been running away from it but now, when he could lose her, he knew a life without her and Emma was no life at all.

The realisation added strength and soon he was back in the cave. By now there was no longer a gap between the top of the cave entrance and the cave and Mac had to take a deep gulp of air and swim underwater. His lungs were bursting as he once more emerged into the cave. To his horror he saw that the water was now up to Emma's waist, even though she was standing on the ledge. Abby was treading water nearby.

'Emma, we have to go now. You, too, Abby,' Mac said, trying to keep his voice even.

Emma was staring, her eyes wide with fear. 'I can't,' she said. 'I've hurt my arm.'

'Yes, you can, my love. Mac and I will each take one side of you. And we'll help you through. We won't let anything happen to you, I promise,' Abby said.

Mac marvelled at Abby. The fear was gone from her voice. It was steady and calm, as if she was suggesting a walk in the park.

'We'll be underwater for thirty seconds. But your mum and I will be on either side of you. All you have to do is keep as still as you can and let us pull you along. Can you do that?' he said.

'Yes,' Emma replied.

'Good girl. But we have to go now.' Mac slid back into the water. Abby held onto Emma's good arm as she slipped into the water and then she jumped in beside them. Mac's heart lurched. Getting through the channel, swimming against the incoming current, would be a challenge. But what choice did they have?

'Okay. On my count of three, we're all going to take a deep breath and then go under. Okay?'

Abby and Emma nodded.

'One, two, three,' Mac said, and then between them he and Abby had Emma. He gripped Emma around the waist, careful to avoid her injured arm. To his relief, the rising tide meant that the current wasn't as strong as it had been. But still he felt every second of the time they spent underwater. True to her word, Emma relaxed, letting them pull her along.

At last, when he thought Emma wouldn't be able to hold her breath any longer, they broke through into the fresh air. The three of them trod water, breathing in deep lungfuls of fresh, clean air, and then the lifeboat was beside them and men were dropping into the water, helping them lift Emma gently onto the boat.

As soon as they were all safely on board, the boat

sped off towards the shore. Over the top of Emma's head Mac and Abby shared a look. In Abby's eyes there was relief and gratitude and something else—love. Soon, when all this was over, he would tell her about the DNA test, but all that mattered right now was that he had his small precious family safe and well beside him.

CHAPTER SIXTEEN

'I was scared,' Emma said, 'but I remembered what Dad told me once and that helped me stay calm.' She was sitting on the hospital trolley. Her arm had been X-rayed and, as they'd expected, found to be broken. It had been put in a cast but the staff wanted to keep in her in overnight for observation. The bruise that was blossoming on her forehead suggested she had knocked her head, too.

'And what was that, darling?' Abby asked.

'He told me that panic kills more people than anything else. He said if you use your head, there is always a way out of most problems. So that's what I did.'

Abby slid a glance at Mac. Emma was more her father's daughter than she had realised. 'When Simon fell, I knew he had hurt his leg quite badly and I knew we couldn't walk out of the cave together. Not through the tide. So I climbed down to stay with him. But I had to get help. My mobile wasn't working. I could hear you, Mum. Some of the words, at least, but not everything. I didn't know for sure if you could hear me.

'I waded out, the tide wasn't so high then, and I waved my arms until I got someone's attention. Then I went back to stay with Simon.' Her voice trembled slightly. 'But on the way I fell over a rock that I couldn't see in the water and bumped my head. I think that's when I hurt my arm.'

'You were very brave. It must have been difficult to climb back up to Simon with only one arm.'

Why didn't you stay out of the cave once you got out? Abby wanted to ask. But she knew the answer. Her heart swelled with pride. Abby hadn't wanted to leave her friend alone and hurt by himself. As Mac had pointed out, she couldn't change her daughter's nature. And despite everything she had been through in the last hour or two, she wouldn't change her daughter for the world.

Eventually, Emma closed her eyes, the exhaustion and the excitement of the last few hours catching up with her.

Abby reached for Mac's hand as they watched her breathing deeply. To her surprise he didn't pull away. Instead, he brought her hand to his mouth and kissed each finger tenderly.

'My God, Abby. For a moment I thought I was going to lose you and Emma. Don't ever do anything like that to me again.' His voice was ragged.

'Don't want to have to train a new teammate?' she said lightly.

'I don't want to lose the woman I love,' Mac replied quietly.

Abby's heart kicked against her ribs. He'd said he loved her. Did he mean as a friend or a lover? She had to know. Silently she waited for him to go on.

'Two months ago I thought I was happy. I had a job I loved, a decent place to live where I could do the sports I enjoy whenever I wanted. It was a good life, a perfect life, until you walked into it.'

Abby couldn't stop her smile. He sounded almost

annoyed. But she knew his life had been empty of all that was important, even if he didn't.

'And then I found out I had a child. This child.' He bent over and kissed Emma gently on the cheek. 'At first I could hardly take it in. I didn't want it to be true. Emma would be nothing except a duty and while I knew I couldn't ignore my responsibilities, I never thought that she would become such an important part of my life. And as for you...' He sighed. 'You drove me insane almost from the moment I set eyes on you. Not just those cat eyes, or that mouth that just cries out to be kissed, or your body, which would make most women weep— those are the things that counted in my other life, but as I got to know you, I realised I was falling hard for you. And it frightened me.' He half smiled. 'That was a new one for me. I didn't think I was scared of anything but I was. I was scared of being in love.'

A warm glow was spreading upwards from her toes and surrounding her heart like a blanket. But she still couldn't be certain he was saying what she so desperately wanted to hear.

'I thought if I took you to bed, that would break the spell. But I was wrong. If anything, I wanted more. I wanted nights and nights with you. I couldn't imagine a time when I would no longer want you. Then you told me you loved me and that frightened me even more. What if I couldn't live up to your expectations of me? What if I let you—and Emma—down? What if I turned out to be like my father? I'd be dragging you and Em down with me. I couldn't do that. I tried to stay away from you, Abby. I wanted you to find someone else, even if the thought ripped me apart. And if it meant losing Emma, too, I knew the man you chose would be a good man. Someone who would love Emma the way she deserved.'

'Do you still believe that?' Abby clasped her hands together to stop herself from reaching out and pushing a wayward lock of hair out of his eyes. Didn't he know that she would never love another man as long as she lived?

'No. I don't. I came close to losing you and Emma today. I knew then that I couldn't let you go. I'm not strong enough to do that.'

Abby came and crouched by his side. Taking his hands in hers, she looked up into his eyes. 'You are the strongest man I know, Mac. In the truest sense of the word. You are not your father. And even if you were I would still take my chances with you. I would rather have a tempestuous life with you than one without you.'

He stood up abruptly, forcing her to drop her hands. 'But that's not all. The lab that took our DNA for testing called today. That's why I was on my way to see you.'

A tendril of fear curled around her heart. The look in Mac's eyes told her something was far from right.

He lowered his voice. 'Abby, Emma is not my child.'

'What?'

'Whatever Sara told you, Abby is not mine.'

Abby's head was reeling. 'But why did she say you were?' As soon as she said the words she guessed the truth. Sara probably hadn't been sure who the father was and that was why she hadn't wanted to give Abby a name at first. But when she'd known she was going to die, she'd given Abby the name of the man she would have liked most to be the father of her child, Mac. Perhaps in her heart she had harboured a dream that once her child was born, she would go to Mac and persuade him Emma was his. They would never know.

'Whoever the biological father of Emma is, it isn't me.'

The pain and disappointment in his eyes shook her. What now? What would he do? There was no reason for him to continue with the relationship. He would walk out of Emma's life and what would that do to Emma?

'Emma's going to be devastated. She adores you. She's so proud to call you her father.'

Mac's jaw tightened. 'No prouder than I was to think she was my daughter. And I love her.' A small smile curled his lips. 'I never thought the day would come when I'd say that.' The smile faded from his eyes. 'I don't care what the test says. I don't care who the biological father is. Damn it, Abby, Emma is my daughter. I don't want to lose her.' He looked away. Emma was still sleeping peacefully.

He reached out and took Abby's hand and pulled her to her feet.

'Come with me. There's something I want to show you.'

'But, Emma... I don't want to leave her.'

'She'll be out for the count for an hour or two. We won't be that long. I'll ask them to bleep me the minute she wakes up.'

Abby hesitated.

'Please, Abby.'

She couldn't resist the appeal in his blue eyes. He was hurting.

She followed him out to the car park. He opened the door to his Jeep and helped her in.

'I don't suppose you're going to tell me where you're taking me?' she said.

He smiled at her and her heart cracked. She loved him so much it hurt. She would have given anything for Emma to be his child.

They drove in silence, turning onto the track where Mac had taken her a few weeks earlier. Abby was baffled. As they drove they passed diggers and lorries. There was obviously work going on.

Mac helped Abby out of the car.

'You and Emma are everything I wanted. I just didn't know it. I love you both.' He turned to Abby, pinning her with the intensity in his blue eyes. 'I'm in love with you, Abby. I'm not good at finding the words, but I know I couldn't bear to live without you. I want to wake up every morning with you beside me and I want yours to be the last face I see when I go to sleep. I want to live my life with you and Emma by my side. I want to have breakfast and dinner with you and Em, take you to Tiree to show you the place I grew up. The works.'

Abby's heart started to pound.

'I thought I could run from you. But I couldn't. I wouldn't let myself accept that I was falling for you.' He smiled sadly. 'Thinking I was a father was shock enough and even though it turned out to be the best thing that ever happened to me, I didn't know if I could commit myself to a wife. All I knew was that I didn't want to let you go.'

He gestured to the building site. 'When you refused to let me build this house for you, I thought I would build it anyway. I began to realise that I was putting down roots. Then, when I was discussing the plans with the architect, I saw the little sitting room with you in it, looking out to sea, a book in your hand. The garden where you would grow your roses. The kitchen where we would eat, the bedroom where I would fall asleep with you in my arms and the starlight shining in the window. Everywhere I looked, there you were. You and Emma. My family. My heart. My reason for living.'

He reached out and tipped her chin so she was looking into his eyes. 'Abby, I love you. I want you to marry me. I want you and Emma to be my family. I know she's not my biological child and that one day she might want to find her real father, but until then, could you love me enough to spend the rest of your life with me?'

A frisson of joy was spreading through Abby's body. Happiness swelled inside her. He loved her. But she had to be sure that this wasn't his way of hanging onto Emma.

'I'll never stop you seeing Em, whatever the results of the test say, and as long as she wants you in her life, which, knowing Em, is going to be for ever. You do know that, Mac?'

He glared at her. 'You don't think I'm saying all this simply because of Em, do you?' He smiled grimly. 'I love you. Heart and soul. For ever. I want babies with you, to grow old with you. To laugh with you. Argue, too, if it comes to that.' He pulled her into his arms. 'I love you, Abby Stevens. Will you get that into your stubborn head?'

The blood was singing through her veins. The way he was looking at her left no doubt in her mind. She brought her face up to his. 'For heaven's sake, how long do I have to wait for my fiancé to kiss me, then?'

And then he was kissing her as if he would never let her go, and she knew at last they had both found the place they were meant to be.

* * *

Emma was just waking up when they tiptoed back into her cubicle. One look at their faces must have told her something was up.

'Hey, what's going on with you two?' she asked.

Mac and Abby sat on the bed on either side of Emma, careful not to bump her injured arm.

'We have two things to tell you. Both are surprises. The first you're going to have to prepare yourself for, the second we think you'll like.'

Emma eyed them warily. Then she broke into a wide smile. 'I know what one of the surprises is,' she said. 'You two are getting married. Am I right?'

'You are. But how did you guess?' Abby said.

'Grown-ups can be so silly,' Emma said scornfully. 'I knew you were in love ages ago. Anybody, even a kid like me...' she slid Abby a mocking glance '...could see it a mile away. Even if you are old.'

Abby and Mac laughed. 'Hey, we're not that old,' Mac protested. 'There's still a few years before we get really ancient.'

'So you're okay with us getting married?' Abby asked.

There was no need for a reply. The smile that lit up Emma's face was all the answer Abby needed. 'I wished you would get married. Does that mean we'll all live together? For ever? Like a real family? I'll have my mum and my dad just like all the other children?'

Despite her happiness, Abby felt a chill. It was going to be a blow to Emma finding out Mac wasn't her biological father.

'Emma,' Mac said, taking her hand. 'I have something to tell you. But first I want you to know that I couldn't love you more than I do now.'

The smile left Emma's face. 'What's going on?' she whispered. She clutched Abby's hand again.

'Remember that test we had? To prove I was your dad?'

'When you and me went to the hospital?'

'Yes, that one.' He took a deep breath and Abby knew he was having difficulty finding the right words. 'It turns out that I'm not your father. At least, I never made you.'

'You mean it wasn't your sperm with my real mummy's eggs?'

Mac looked so shocked that Abby had to laugh. 'I've always told Emma the truth. And it seemed silly to wait until some other child gave her the wrong information. Emma knows how babies are made. At least,' she rushed on, in case Mac misunderstood, 'the biological basis.'

Emma frowned. 'I thought you said people made babies when they loved each other. But my real mum didn't even know who my father was.'

Oh, dear. Abby thought. This was going to take some explaining...

Luckily Mac stepped in. 'Your mum, Sara, was a kind, lovely person. But she was a little lonely. Sometimes people make babies because they want someone to love and look after. I think that's why Sara made you. Whoever your real father is, your mother made you out of love.'

'And you always have to remember that,' Abby said softly. 'She loved you more than anything in the world. So much she didn't want to share you.'

'But if Mac's not my real dad...' Emma's lip trembled and tears spilled down her cheek '...then we're not really a family.'

'Emma, look at me,' Mac said firmly. He waited until

Emma turned her blue eyes to his. Abby's throat tightened when she saw the trust there. 'You and Abby are
my family. I love you both more than anything in the
world. I want to be your dad for as long as you'll let me.
I want to be the one who chases the boyfriends away,
who picks you up from parties.' His voice softened.
'Who walks you up the aisle. We can carry on looking
for your real dad, but if you let me, us...' he turned to
Abby '...we want to adopt you, so you really belong to
us. What do you say?'

Emma cuddled into Mac, snuggling deep into his
arms. He stroked her hair, comforting her.

'I say yes,' Emma said. Then she pulled away and
took hold of Abby's hand, too. 'So does that mean I can
go to night-time parties now?'

EPILOGUE

ABBY stood by the window of her new home. In the sitting room, her mother and Mac's were chatting ninety to the dozen, each trying to outdo the other. Mac's mother had come down for the wedding and although she had grumbled about being away from Tiree almost constantly since she had got to Cornwall, Abby suspected she was pleased and touched that Mac had asked her to come to their wedding. Two more days then she'd be walking down the aisle with Mac, and she still couldn't believe it.

She felt his arm slip around her waist and she leaned against him, savouring the warmth and security of his embrace.

'Happy?' he whispered into her ear.

She nodded. Two more days and he'd be coming to live with her and Emma. He had refused to move in before, saying he wanted to wait until after they married. The house was everything he had told her it would be. Although enormous windows captured the view from every side, it was still cosy.

'You must come to Tiree to visit me,' Mac's mother was saying. 'I don't live in a grand house like this,' she sniffed, but Abby was beginning to realise that she didn't mean half of what she said, 'or in London, where all the fancy people live, but my house is good enough for me.'

'Your house is so sweet, Gran MacNeil,' Emma protested. 'I love it. Especially the chickens. And so is yours, Grandma Stevens,' she added hastily.

Abby smiled. Emma was ever the diplomat. Whatever differences the two older women had with their own children, there was no doubt they doted on their grandchild. Indeed, they spent all their time trying to compete for her affection.

Behind her, she heard Mac stifle a laugh. He had learned to be tolerant of both parents. 'At the very least,' he had told Abby, 'we both know how not to do it.'

Emma left the two old women to their bickering and came to stand next to Abby. She was to be bridesmaid at their wedding and was barely able to control her excitement about having a brother or sister to boss around in a few months' time. Mac reached across to pull her into the circle of his embrace.

'My two best girls,' he said. 'My daughter and my wife-to-be.' Mac and Abby had formally adopted Emma. His voice turned serious. 'Have I told you both that I consider myself to be the luckiest man alive?'

Emma giggled. 'Only all the time. You're so sad, Dad.'

He placed a proprietorial hand on Abby's stomach, where her body was just beginning to swell with her pregnancy.

'No, not that. Not any more.'

Abby raised her face to his. She never got over seeing her love reflected in his eyes.

'I have the best life,' Emma sighed happily.

'The best life. That's what we have. No one could be luckier.'

Together they watched as the sun melted into the sea.

are proud to present our...

Book of the Month

Walk on the Wild Side
by Natalie Anderson

from Mills & Boon® RIVA™

Jack Greene has Kelsi throwing caution to the wind
—it's hard to stay grounded with a man who turns
your world upside down! Until they crash with
a bump—of the baby kind...

Available 4th February

*Something to say about our Book of the Month?
Tell us what you think!*

millsandboon.co.uk/community
facebook.com/romancehq
twitter.com/millsandboonuk

ULTIMATE ALPHA MALES:
Strong, sexy…and intent on seduction!

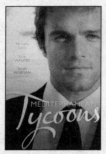

Mediterranean Tycoons
4th February 2011

Hot-Shot Heroes
4th March 2011

Powerful Protectors
1st April 2011

Passionate Playboys
6th May 2011

Collect all four!
www.millsandboon.co.uk

Nora Roberts' *The O'Hurleys*

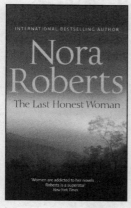

4th March 2011

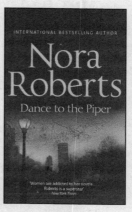

1st April 2011

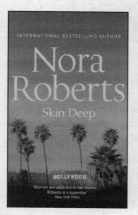

6th May 2011

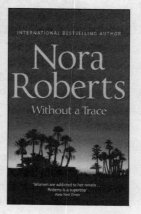

3rd June 2011

www.millsandboon.co.uk

How far would you go to protect your sister?

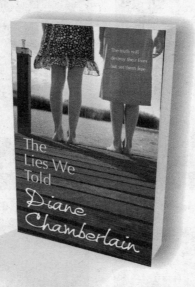

As teenagers, Maya and Rebecca Ward witnessed
their parents' murder. Now doctors, Rebecca has
become the risk taker whilst her sister Maya lives a
quiet life with her husband Adam, unwilling to deal
with her secrets from the night her parents died.

When a hurricane hits North Carolina, Maya is
feared dead. As hope fades, Adam and Rebecca
face unexpected feelings. And Rebecca finds
some buried secrets of her own.

2 FREE BOOKS
AND A SURPRISE GIFT

We would like to take this opportunity to thank you for reading this Mills & Boon® book by offering you the chance to take TWO more specially selected books from the Modern™ series absolutely FREE! We're also making this offer to introduce you to the benefits of the Mills & Boon® Book Club™—

- **FREE home delivery**
- **FREE gifts and competitions**
- **FREE monthly Newsletter**
- **Exclusive Mills & Boon Book Club offers**
- **Books available before they're in the shops**

Accepting these FREE books and gift places you under no obligation to buy, you may cancel at any time, even after receiving your free books. Simply complete your details below and return the entire page to the address below. You don't even need a stamp!

YES Please send me 2 free Modern books and a surprise gift. I understand that unless you hear from me, I will receive 4 superb new books every month for just £3.30 each, postage and packing free. I am under no obligation to purchase any books and may cancel my subscription at any time. The free books and gift will be mine to keep in any case.

Ms/Mrs/Miss/Mr _____ Initials _____

Surname _____

Address _____

_____ Postcode _____

E-mail _____

Send this whole page to: Mills & Boon Book Club, Free Book Offer, FREEPOST NAT 10298, Richmond, TW9 1BR

Offer valid in UK only and is not available to current Mills & Boon Book Club subscribers to this series. Overseas and Eire please write for details.. We reserve the right to refuse an application and applicants must be aged 18 years or over. Only one application per household. Terms and prices subject to change without notice. Offer expires 30th April 2011. As a result of this application, you may receive offers from Harlequin Mills & Boon and other carefully selected companies. If you would prefer not to share in this opportunity please write to The Data Manager, PO Box 676, Richmond, TW9 1WU.

Mills & Boon® is a registered trademark owned by Harlequin Mills & Boon Limited.
Modern™ is being used as a trademark. The Mills & Boon® Book Club™ is being used as a trademark.